P9-ASI-709

"Come on, Katie, dance with me," Matthew challenged her.

But when the next song on the radio proved to be a slow ballad full of romance and emotion, she backed away. "I never learned to slow dance," she lied.

He saw through her and wasn't having any of it. "Then it's past time you learned."

Feeling just a little threatened by all that masculine appeal, all that sensual heat he was directing point-blank at her, she hesitated. "The cookies—"

"Are fine," he said, checking the timer. "We've got five minutes, Katie. I can teach you a lot in five minutes."

She'd just bet he could—and would. Wearing a look that clearly warned *Resist me and see where it gets you*, he gently took her wrist and pulled her flush against him.

"The thing about slow dancing," he whispered, "is that you can make it anything you want it to be. A dance . . ." He moved slowly, sensuously against her. "An adventure . . ." His hands glided down her back. "Or a seduction . . ."

WHAT ARE *LOVESWEPT* ROMANCES?

They are stories of true romance and touching emotion. We believe those two very important ingredients are constants in our highly sensual and very believable stories in the LOVESWEPT *line. Our goal is to give you, the reader, stories of consistently high quality that may sometimes make you laugh, sometimes make you cry, but are always fresh and creative and contain many delightful surprises within their pages.*

Most romance fans read an enormous number of books. Those they truly love, they keep. Others may be traded with friends and soon forgotten. We hope that each LOVESWEPT *romance will be a treasure—a "keeper." We will always try to publish*

LOVE STORIES YOU'LL NEVER FORGET
BY AUTHORS YOU'LL ALWAYS REMEMBER

The Editors

MAN AROUND
THE HOUSE

CINDY
GERARD

BANTAM BOOKS
NEW YORK · TORONTO · LONDON · SYDNEY · AUCKLAND

MAN AROUND THE HOUSE
A Bantam Book / July 1993

LOVESWEPT® *and the wave design are registered*
trademarks of Bantam Books, a division of
Bantam Doubleday Dell Publishing Group, Inc.
Registered in U.S. Patent
and Trademark Office and elsewhere.

All rights reserved.
Copyright © 1993 by Cindy Gerard.
Cover art copyright © 1993 by Lina Levy.
No part of this book may be reproduced or transmitted
in any form or by any means, electronic or mechanical,
including photocopying, recording, or by any
information storage and retrieval system, without
permission in writing from the publisher.
For information address: Bantam Books.

If you purchased this book without a cover you should be aware that this
book is stolen property. It was reported as "unsold and destroyed" to the
publisher and neither the author nor the publisher has received any
payment for this "stripped book."

If you would be interested in receiving protective vinyl covers for your
Loveswept books, please write to this address for information:

Loveswept
Bantam Books
P.O. Box 985
Hicksville, NY 11802

ISBN 0-553-44297-X

Published simultaneously in the United States and Canada

Bantam Books are published by Bantam Books, a division of Bantam Dou-
bleday Dell Publishing Group, Inc. Its trademark, consisting of the words
"Bantam Books" and the portrayal of a rooster, is Registered in U.S. Patent
and Trademark Office and in other countries. Marca Registrada. Bantam
Books, 1540 Broadway, New York, New York 10036.

PRINTED IN THE UNITED STATES OF AMERICA

OPM   0 9 8 7 6 5 4 3 2 1

To the charter members of the Hearts Club,
Karen, Carole, and Denise.
Thanks for all the grief, all the guff,
and all the giggles.

MAN AROUND
THE HOUSE

ONE

All her life Katie McDonald had been warned: Cats with less curiosity than she hadn't made it past two of their allotted nine lives. Couple that particular character trait with her notorious errors in judgment, and the general consensus was that one day she'd do herself in.

Today appeared to be the day. The prophecy was finally going to come true.

Not that she didn't deserve to be in this fix. She did. It was just that she'd always thought that when her time came, she'd go down in a great blaze of glory, her life snuffed out like the flame of a flickering candle as she boldly went where no consumer advocate had gone before and, in the process, sacrificed her life to the cause.

Apparently that climactic scene wasn't in the cards. It seemed she'd just been dealt her final hand, and it was playing like a cheap game of strip poker.

Naked as a saturated jaybird, Katie sagged deeper into her bathtub and wondered distractedly if a person could die from overexposure to bubbles and tepid bath water. By rights, drowning—poetically appropriate to the situation—would do the trick. She'd already ruled that out, though, because she really didn't want to get her hair wet.

She eyed her big toe, which she'd decided about a half an hour ago was wedged for eternity—or forever, whichever came first—inside her bathtub faucet.

She'd lost track of how long she'd been stuck this way. Long enough, she knew, that with the exception of her captive toe, every other part of her body was shriveling. Prunes should look so good.

Calling on her dwindling power of concentration, she tried to will the stubborn critter free. When that approach didn't work any better than the others, she narrowed her eyes, gritted her teeth, and out of sheer desperation, gave a mighty tug. Pain shot all the way to her ankle, yet still her swollen toe refused to budge.

Leaning back in defeat, she muttered a disgusted "Damn." Because it felt so good, she said it again, this time with feeling. For good measure she gave the water a slap. A showering spray hit her full in the face.

Snapping her mouth shut, she swiped a cascade of bubbles from her eyes and cursed the day she'd ever seen the rerun of that old sitcom. She'd laughed back then at the ridiculous premise. She wasn't laughing now.

Like the star of the show, she'd had a hard day and decided to treat herself to a hot bath before dinner. She'd lain back and relaxed, enjoying the steaming water, the luxurious bubbles, and the subtle scent of a new bath salts she'd splurged on called Spring Sunset. Then she'd made her fatal error. Was it really possible, she'd wondered, grinning, to get your big toe stuck in a faucet?

She wasn't wondering anymore. And she wasn't grinning.

Not only was it possible, the odds of it happening were roughly the same as the odds of Erma Bombeck making a crack about her age, her weight, or the fuzzy green things growing in her refrigerator. Katie's big toe was stuck tighter than tights on an overweight ballerina.

"It's no use," she moaned miserably, and sank deeper into despair. "Help," she cried for the umpteenth time, straining to cast her voice out the high bathroom window. "Help, help, help, already! Can't anybody hear me?"

"Lady, I hear you, but where the devil are you?"

Katie yelped when the deep masculine voice boomed in the bathroom. Sloshing lower into the tub, she frantically and futilely tried to cover up before it dawned on her that he, whoever he was, was standing *outside* the house, beneath her bathroom window. He couldn't see her any more than she could see him.

"Are you all right in there?" he asked.

"Fine," she squeaked, spitting out bubbles. "Just . . . fine."

Heart racing, she frowned toward the window. The silence told her he was probably frowning too.

"Umm, ma'am?"

The rich, rumbling voice drifting into the bathroom managed to make her feel even more exposed. "Yes?"

"That was *you* calling for help, wasn't it?"

"I, uh . . ." She swallowed, knowing where this was leading and not knowing how to avoid it. "Yes," she admitted dismally. "It was me."

"Well, is there anything I can do to help you?"

Katie crossed her fingers and shot for the moon. "You could tell me you're the neighbor lady and you've got a bad chest cold."

"I beg your pardon?"

She sighed, resigned to the reality. Before she'd even asked, she'd known that a voice like that could only belong to someone who had intimate knowledge of men's locker rooms, five-o-clock shadows, and power drills. "Never mind. I . . . I'm afraid I really could use a little help here."

"Name it," he said. His voice held a sensuality that

had her associating him with midnight, satin sheets, a carton of chocolate ice cream and a single spoon.

She shivered at the erotic rush that picture created. Dementia had obviously set in. She had to get out of there. Fast. And to do that, there was nothing for it but to come out with it.

"This is really a little silly," she began, affecting a gee-aren't-I-just-the-one tone, "but I seem to have gotten myself stuck in here."

"Stuck?"

The inflection he managed to place on that one word shredded the thin hope that she might get out of this with her dignity intact.

She scowled at her uncooperative toe. "I'd say 'stuck' pretty well sums it up."

"Stuck how, exactly?"

She couldn't admit it. She just couldn't. Twenty years from now, *maybe* she could look back and laugh. At this very moment, having her food sent in until she figured out a solution was a supremely appealing option. "Look. I don't want to impose on you, but if you could just make a phone call for me? My friend can come over and help." She rattled off Rachael's number.

"That's a Liberty prefix, isn't it? Liberty's clear across town, a good hour away. Seems silly to wait that long when I'm right here and perfectly willing to help."

He was right, and his practicality made her situation seem all the more ludicrous. But despite popular opinion, and current circumstances, she was a cautious person. Sometimes. After all, she didn't even know this guy's name or, for that matter, if he was a neighbor or just made a habit of skulking around backyards with breaking and entering on his mind. And to consider letting him into her house just because he had a lay-me-down-and-do-things-to-me voice didn't mean she was willing to lay herself down and let him.

And where had that come from, Katherine Irene McDonald? she asked herself in disgust. The fact that she was even thinking along those lines—if only fleetingly—spoke volumes about her soggy state of mind.

"Maybe this would be a little easier for you if I introduced myself," he said, unintentionally making matters worse by having the sensitivity to understand her misgivings. "I'm one of your new neighbors, Matthew Spencer. I'd heard this place had been sold and that someone had moved in, but I was out of town until yesterday, so I haven't had a chance to come see you and welcome you to the neighborhood."

She looked down the wet length of her body. It seemed unavoidable that he was about to see her soon. Great gobs of her. And he was wrong. Nothing was going to make it easier.

"Hey, are you still with me in there?"

Like she could possibly go somewhere?

She scowled at her foot, suspended from the faucet like a sausage in a butcher shop. If she could have pulled the plug and slithered down the drain with the bathwater, she'd have cheerfully done it. But there was the toe to consider. It seemed particularly attached to her foot. She muttered an expletive under her breath.

"I'm sorry, I missed that."

She let out a fatalistic sigh. "I said, don't worry. I'm not going anywhere. It's nice to meet you, Matthew. I'm Katie McDonald and someday when this is a memory, I'm going to be very glad you came to my rescue."

"It's nice to meet you too, Katie. Now what can I do?"

She took one last stab at avoiding what now seemed to be inevitable. "There wouldn't happen to be a *Mrs.* Spencer around somewhere, would there?"

"We don't got a Mrs. Spencer," a new and obviously young male voice piped up. "It's just me and Dad."

Just me and Dad, Katie thought, mulling over the possible reasons for that scenario. It was now two to one, and she could kiss the hope of female camaraderie good-bye.

"Sorry, Katie," Matthew added. "Looks like you're stuck with Joey and me."

She groaned. "I'm going to pretend you didn't say that."

He laughed. The sound was as sensual and as tummy tightening as his voice.

"You want to tell me exactly what the problem is?"

he asked. "My imagination is doing cartwheels trying to pin this down. And I'm starting to feel a little silly standing here talking to a window."

He couldn't begin to comprehend the meaning of the word "silly," she thought. And if she could have ignored the fact that her skin had taken on the tint and texture of wet elephant hide, she might have pressed him again to call Rachael before he discovered what silly really was. But she wanted out. Preferably before Halley's comet made another appearance.

She hung her head, giving up and giving in. The hell with death before dishonor. Now was not the time to look a gift rescuer in the mouth.

"Let's just hope your imagination has a sense of humor," she said, tasting the bitterness of the pride she swallowed. "I lost mine about two hours ago."

Katie had to give Matthew credit. He didn't laugh when she told him about her toe. At least not so that she could hear him. What he did was take charge. After telling him where to find her extra house key in the garage, he let himself into the house.

The last of the bathwater was gurgling down the drain when he rapped a knuckle on the bathroom door. "How's it going? You hanging in there?"

"You have an uncanny knack for phrasing," she said.

"Sorry."

She heard the grin in his voice and couldn't even fault him for it.

"I don't suppose there's a chance this door is unlocked?" he said.

She sighed deeply, scooping all the bubbles she could gather and considering where to stack them. "That would be too easy, now, wouldn't it?"

"Hey, no sweat. I love a challenge. Just sit tight. I'll go grab my toolbox and be right back. Joey, why don't you stay here and keep the lady company?"

Joey did just that, reassuring and regaling her with a five-year-old's account of his father's prowess as a hero of epic proportions.

He was just getting into an in-depth probe of why she'd stuck her toe in the faucet, when Matthew returned and saved her from the equivalent of the Spanish Inquisition.

"Here we go," Matthew said cheerfully. "I'll just screw off the doorknob and we'll have it open in no time."

"Don't worry, Katie," Joey added with enthusiastic reassurance. "My dad's a real good screwer. Right, Dad?"

On the other side of the door, Matthew cleared his throat. Loudly. For the first time in several hours Katie felt like grinning.

"And he's got all the right tools too. Right, Dad?"

The throat clearing turned into a hearty cough.

She couldn't help it. A laugh bubbled out. All the right tools, huh? She settled back in the tub as the mellow, sensual sound of James Taylor's "Handy Man" drifted through her mind.

A few minutes later the doorknob bounced to the floor. "That does it," Matthew said. "What's the situation, Katie? Are you up to having a little company in there?"

She glanced at the bare rod she hadn't yet had time to hang with a shower curtain, at the towels on the rack a good arm's length out of reach, and finally at her bathrobe, hanging even farther away on the back of the door. "I'm up for an even break, but I wouldn't make book on the odds of it coming through."

She ran a final check on the washcloth she'd draped carefully over her lower anatomy, her arms strategically crossed over her breasts, and the rapidly popping bubbles she'd tucked in what she thought were rather creative clumps over other critical locations. She was as prepared as she could get.

He's a father, she reminded herself. If the hero worship evident in Joey's voice was any indication, he was a good one. A good father would not, especially in front of his child, try any funny stuff. Even if he did have all the right tools.

"My robe's on the back of the door," she said. "Maybe you could just sort of toss it to me?"

"Sure thing," he replied breezily, as if they weren't both thinking about the fact that she was birthday-suit bare.

Getting ahold of her robe, however, was easier said than done.

The door opened marginally. She sank a little lower and watched as a large, strong-fingered, and very tanned hand snaked inside and groped for her robe. Either the door was too wide or the arm was too short. Of course.

"I can't seem to reach it."

"Why does that not surprise me?"

"How about if I—"

That fabulous voice stopped mid-question when Joey—she assumed it was Joey—came quickly and unexpectedly to the rescue. Slipping through the narrow opening, the little boy scooted inside.

"Hi," he said shyly when he caught sight of her in the tub.

Feeling as exposed as a chicken in a stew pot, she pinched out a pained smile, wiggled two fingers in greeting, and prayed for invisibility.

In his Kansas City Royals T-shirt and cutoffs, Joey looked like a living endorsement for the benefits of all the food groups. His cheeks glowed rosy pink, his straight corn-silk blond hair shone under the glow of the vanity light, his brown eyes danced with inquisitiveness, and his stocky little limbs supported a pint-sized powerhouse of boundless energy.

His bashful smile faded to a frown as his gaze slid from her face, down the length of bubbles, and finally to her toe. "I thought you were teasing. I thought she was teasing, Dad!" he yelled back toward the door. "But she's not. She really does got her toe stuck in the faucet."

Clasping his little hands together on the top of his head, Joey scowled down at her as if she'd set the Guiness record for stupidity. "Didn't your dad ever tell you not to stick your toe in a faucet?"

It hurt to be dressed down by a five-year-old, but she took it like a trooper.

"And didn't I tell you it's not polite to ask so many questions?" his father asked pointedly.

"But, gee, Dad—"

"Enough, bud. We're here to help the lady, not kill her with questions. Can you reach her robe?"

He could, although it took a little jumping and finagling to tug it off the hook. Katie grinned at his antics.

"I got it."

"Way to go, squirt. Now hand it to Katie and come back out here while she puts it on."

Shy again after Katie offered her praise and thanks, Joey scooted out the door.

Small favor that it was, Katie thanked the powers that be for bestowing her with a penchant for heavy, floor-length terry cloth bathrobes. She squirmed into the soft red cotton and breathed a sigh of relief—that was cut short when she heard Joey giggle on the other side of the door and confide to his dad, "She's got bubbles on her tummy."

Katie rolled her eyes heavenward. What was left of her good humor was popping like said bubbles as she imagined her hero, "Hardware Hank," imagining the bubbles on her tummy. If he laughed, if there was so much as a hint of a smile when he uttered the inevitable "Are you decent yet?" she was going to growl.

"Are you decent yet?" he asked on cue, waited a heartbeat, then added warily, "Is there a dog in there?"

She counted to ten. "No dog. Just a temper that has grown to beastly proportions." Making a quick check to see if all the important parts were covered, she looked toward the door. "Be my guest. Please. Come on in."

She'd decided, since she'd first heard his voice, that she knew exactly what he looked like. Voices rarely matched faces and forms. She'd learned that long ago.

Back in the days when she'd still believed in such nonsense as romance, she'd had a monumental crush on a deejay whose velvety rasp of a voice had raised the pulse rates and fleshed out the fantasies of hundreds of women in the Kansas City listening area. When she'd actually met the man, her illusions had shattered like a windshield connecting with a foul ball.

She worked real hard at envisioning Matthew Spencer as a clone of that deejay: What shoulders he had would be stooped, what hair he had would be sprouting from his nose and ears, and the closest he would come to exemplifying the rugged virility of the Marlboro man would be the wishbone bow of his legs.

But when he finally opened the door and stepped inside, she discovered she was far off the mark.

Life was not fair. And Matthew Spencer wasn't within a meteor's toss of Mr. Midnight of KCMO radio.

What Matthew Spencer was, was gorgeous. Not drop-dead, poster-perfect, to-die-for gorgeous. Oh, no. It was worse. Much worse. He was an unsettling combination of boy-next-door and hard-knocks gorgeous, devil-be-damned and every-mother-loves-him gorgeous, that left no doubt about the kind of man she was dealing with. He was a heartbreaker.

She could see it in the way he wore his wheat-colored hair. A little too long, a little too mussed, the casual style clearly stated: *What you see is what I am and however you feel about it is okay by me.*

She could see it in his eyes. They were pepper-mill brown and twinkling with just the right mix of compassion and humor . . . and something else. She sensed a sadness inside him, shadowed and dark, that the smile lines framing those expressive eyes couldn't quite conceal.

As if those particular characteristics weren't enough

to set her pulse racing, there was his mouth to deal with. It couldn't have been hard and cynical, set in a condescending sneer. It had to be full and wide, and so politely reluctant to crack into a grin that his effort tickled her heart from the inside out.

His nose had been broken, she was sure of it. Maybe more than once, she decided upon further inspection. It should have detracted from his features. Instead it enhanced and distinguished them, revealing not only an aching vulnerability, but a resilience that suggested he could take what life dished out and come out the better for it.

With all that going for him, he could have at least had the decency to be out of shape. But there, too, he defied the predictable. Even beneath the gray short-sleeve ARMY sweatshirt and acid-washed denims that sported some dangerously worn areas, she could see this was no sofa slug she was dealing with. The shoulders were broad, the chest muscles toned, the belly lean.

Put it all together and it spelled "man" in the most essential definition of the word. Everything about him had a lived-in, used-hard look that was as disarming as a hand grenade with the pin pulled yet as comfortable as an old shoe. And as sexy as ever-loving sin.

In short, he was a dangerous man. He was trouble. Unfortunately, she was a woman who was attracted to trouble the way *The National Enquirer* was attracted to Donald Trump.

This was not good.

"Oh, please, Scottie," she pleaded to the ceiling. "Beam me aboard."

TWO

Matthew had been prepared for cute. In fact, the situation had actively screamed "Cute" when he'd heard that first frustrated cry for help. Since then, his imagination had been working overtime trying to picture Katie McDonald stranded in her bathtub, in the buff.

Fortunately for both of them, buff wasn't an issue. When he'd finally stepped through the bathroom door, she'd managed to drape herself in yards of red terry cloth and a wavering indignation. *Cute* didn't even begin to cover it.

A pickup truck full of W words came to mind instead: Winsome, wistful, willful, to name a few. Wicked, wild, and willowy, to name a few more. And wet. Definitely wet, he concluded, and threw more effort into fighting a determined grin.

Flashing eyes as blue as bachelor buttons looked

him up and down. "Ace Hardware, I presume?" she said, as sassy as you please.

He gave up the fight and let the grin take over. Touching his screwdriver to his forehead, he gave her a smart salute. "At your service, ma'am."

Then he spotted her foot dangling from the faucet and he lost it. He tried hard not to laugh. He really did. In the end, though, it got the best of him. He covered his mouth with his hand and his chuckle with a cough.

"You really ought to take something for that cold," she said with as much starch as her wilting dignity could allow.

"Just a little something stuck in my throat."

Their gazes snagged. The look in her eyes assured him she knew that "little something" was a laugh and that she was working on forgiving him for it.

"Yeah, well." She nodded toward her toe. " 'Stuck' seems to be the operative word here."

He knew right then that he liked her. In fact, he'd decided as much when he'd first heard her voice, an intriguing mix of kitten softness and gutsy sarcasm. And now that he'd gotten a look at the whole package, he was certain Katie McDonald was one of a kind. She was Kathleen Turner pretty, Lucille Ball ditsy, and still managed to handle a situation as ludicrous as this with Diane Sawyer poise.

It was small wonder, then, with that particular combination of characterizations muddling around in his mind, he still didn't know what to think of her. How *did* one get a make on a woman who'd wedged her big toe in a faucet?

And there was that sneaky little trick she had of making him smile. He hadn't exactly had a lot to smile about the past few years, and he was still in the process of analyzing how she'd managed to squeeze out so many so quickly, when another one slipped right past him.

"So, what do you think, Ace?" she asked. "Is there hope?"

He leaned back out the open door and riffled through his toolbox. When he popped back inside he was sporting a hacksaw and a demented, blood-lusting leer. "Piece of cake."

She sighed theatrically. "Oh, good. And you're a comedian too."

He laughed and settled a hip on the rim of the tub. "Let's take a look," he said, and set about a gentle examination of her trapped toe. "We'll have it out of there in a jiffy."

A jiffy, in this situation, equated to an hour of coaxing, creaming, oiling, praying, and a little creative G-rated cursing over her swollen toe. Joey, patient as a peach ripening in the sun, had a ringside seat on the commode. Watching the goings-on, he offered original and sometimes gruesome suggestions as to how he'd "get that little sucker out of there."

Fortunately, Matthew hit on a solution before they had to resort to the hacksaw or, to Joey's dismay, the dynamite. A Water Pik and hot baby oil finally turned the tide.

Matthew really didn't blame Katie for being cranky. Her toe was sore, her pride was bruised, and, according to the lady, the entire right side of her body had gone into hibernation.

"Quit fussing," he scolded gently as he lifted her, grumbling and ruffled, out of the tub. "You're not going to be able to stand, let alone walk, until you get the circulation back in that leg." He grunted and settled her in his arms as she tugged on her robe and groused about being a helpless twit.

"My, you're a big one, aren't you?" he said.

Actually, she wasn't big at all. She was willow thin and as heavy as moonlight, but he sensed the remark would give her a chance to focus her anger on someone other than herself. She didn't disappoint him. And that earned her another teasing grin. The situation called for teasing and he planned on obliging, although teasing was another activity he hadn't engaged in of late with a woman. That triggered more questions as to why she'd uncovered that lost art in him.

He hefted her closer to his chest as he negotiated the doorway. Though she wasn't heavy, she was long, long and coltishly lean.

"Where to, Katie?" he asked, looking up and down the hall.

"The dumpster."

Scarlett O'Hara couldn't have delivered the line with more dramatic despair. Rhett Butler couldn't have responded with a more roguish grin. "I think we can do better than that."

It wasn't a big house. The floor plan was simple. He found her bedroom with the unerring instincts of a contractor who had built more than his share of modest suburban houses.

He gently laid her down, then fluffed a couple of pillows behind her head. Joey perched on the foot of the bed, propped his chin in his palm, and watched.

"So," Matthew said, trying to make light of the fact that no matter how you sliced it, they were strangers sharing an uncommon intimacy. "Feeling any better?"

She attempted to move her leg, then tried to hide a grimace that showed how much the effort cost her. "If I felt any better, you wouldn't be able to stand me."

Her determined show of pride raised a compassion in him that knocked him for a bit of a loop. And when her restless shifting revealed a glimpse of a smooth white thigh, the sudden stirring in his lower anatomy practically nailed him to the wall.

That's when he admitted he might have a problem.

He'd been determined to ignore them, but the reactions he'd suppressed since he'd found her in her tub grabbed him by the scruff of his neck and shook him until he paid attention.

It had been easy, initially, to tag her with nice generic labels like "klutzy" and "cute," and chalk off his interest as garden-variety curiosity coupled with the need for some comic relief. It was difficult, however, to acknowledge the way she'd felt in his arms—all snuggly female heat and dewy indignation—or the way she looked lying on her bed—all tousled blond topknot and dazzling blue eyes.

And the way she smelled. The fragrance had mesmerized him since he'd first opened her bathroom door. Sweet clover, he decided finally. She smelled of sweet clover and spring rain, a scent as fresh as her mouth and as vibrant as sunshine. It was an oddly intriguing combination that from the beginning had drawn him in the way cookies drew Joey.

Joey was a little boy. He, however, was a man. At thirty-five, he knew how to curb his more base instincts. Determined to do just that, he eased a hip onto the bed and began a businesslike massage of her leg to renew the circulation.

At least it started out as business. It ended up as something else entirely.

It really was a great leg, he thought as he worked through a slow, deep massage. Long, elegant, sleek . . . like the rest of her. She was very nice to touch. Easy to hold, easy on the eye, and hard on his, umm . . . objectivity.

Within a few minutes his therapeutic rubdown had evolved into a hands-on study in satin and symmetry. And sensations. He wasn't sure how it had happened, but four of his five senses had already fired the torpedoes and the fifth was poised on red alert.

Even knowing it was wrong, he became caught up in the feel of the firm, supple length of her leg as he kneaded up and down in a slow, steady rhythm. Her radio, tuned to the oldies station he listened to himself, played softly in the background and didn't help matters in the least. The suggestive lyrics and hot, heavy beat of The Doors' "Light My Fire" added another rhythm, another dimension, and joined the ebb and flow of his hands.

Somehow, in the midst of the massage, the music, and the moment, another W word slipped, unbidden, into his mind: wanton. What, he found himself wondering as his gaze followed his thoughts, would her soft, parted lips taste like?

He met her steady, yet startled gaze and knew she felt the tension too.

She looked both vulnerable and stunningly aware that the pale silk of her leg and the deep tan of his hands formed a contrast they'd each been contemplating. That the slow glide of his palms over her skin had created a tingling friction that was fast edging toward combustion.

The room became very quiet. Too quiet. Too small. And too tense.

"Well," he said, in an effort to shake off the sensual awareness eddying between them. "Does that feel any better?"

Obviously she was having a little trouble with this too. She hardly looked capable of breathing, let alone answering him. He decided not to wait for an answer. Her face said everything for her anyway. Poor thing. She'd lose her shirt in a poker game. And if he let this go on any longer, he wasn't so sure he wouldn't lose something too.

Ignoring the message in her eyes, the sultry words of the song, and his own body's betrayal, he covered her leg with her robe.

With great difficulty he pasted on a fraternal smile, patted her knee, and shot off the bed.

"What do you say, Joey?" He turned to his top priority, wishing his voice wasn't so gruff. "We'd better scoot if we're going to make the first pitch."

Oblivious to the tension, Joey jumped to the floor and headed for the door at the reminder that they had tickets to the Royals baseball game.

Lingering beside the bed, Matthew looked down into Katie's eyes, which were too bright and too telling. What he saw there tempted him to stay. It was a disturbing measure of awareness, an awareness that he suspected mirrored his own.

Get out of here, he ordered himself, knowing much more was at stake than the moment. Yet he stayed, trying to convince himself it was concern keeping him by her side. "You can handle it from here, right, Katie?"

She nodded and managed a sandpapery "Right."

Only there was nothing right about Katie, Matthew thought. Not in his scheme of things. She was wrong. He could feel it with every breath he drew. As wrong as nuclear warfare. Wrong for him. Wrong for Joey.

Pay attention, Spencer, he told himself. The message couldn't read any clearer: Do not buy a ticket to this ride! It would be too wild, too reckless. He had far too much depending on nice and normal to court disaster on a joyride with a woman like her.

He knew all that. So why was he standing there scraping for more reasons not to strap himself in? And why was he so tempted to flirt with the heat of Katie McDonald's fire?

She wasn't even his type. The woman stuck her toes in faucets, for Pete's sake! Besides, he already knew what he needed. Lisa. She was nice, normal, and comfortable. They understood each other. His future with Joey depended on him keeping his feet on level ground. Lisa kept them there. He hadn't come this close to getting Joey back full-time to blow it over a sneak attack of hormonal overload.

Convinced he was anchored again, he braced his hands on his hips and accepted that there was nowhere this could go.

"You going to be okay now?" he asked.

She pinched out a game smile. "I'm fine. Hey, and Joey . . . thanks for coming to my rescue. You, too, Ace," she added, her eyes struggling to regain their sassy twinkle. "The Lone Ranger and Tonto couldn't have done a better job."

He almost asked her then how she felt about baseball. He could see her in tight jeans, a T-shirt, and a baseball cap as she ragged the umpire and tossed peanuts in her mouth.

Her expression, however, stopped him from issuing an invitation. She was struggling with this attraction too; it was written all over that open book she called a face. For her own reasons, she was clearly warning him off.

Yeah, well, that made two of them who knew that whatever the cause for the sparks flying between them, distance was the water that would put them out. He didn't know her reason for wanting to douse them. He only knew his, and it was standing by the door ready to go to a baseball game.

He tossed Katie one last, regretful grin. "You take care, now." Then he hightailed it out the door.

To safer, saner territory.

❦━━━━❦

Two weeks later, as a warm May sun basted his bare shoulders and back, Matthew was not, for the moment at any rate, thinking about his neighbor and how she continually tested his definition of safe and sane. He was concentrating on his son.

The basketball careened off the garage door. He caught it and tossed it back to Joey. "Hey, sport, nice shot! You almost hit the rim that time. You been practicing behind my back and not telling your old man?"

"Gee, Dad. I didn't even come close."

"Sure you did. Michael Jordan would be hanging up his Nikes if he could see your style."

Joey's lips curled up comically to reveal the gaping hole where his two front teeth used to be.

Love swelled inside Matthew's chest. He had to fight the urge to scoop Joey up in his arms and hug him hard. Knowing Joey would consider the display of affection out of the boundary of *guy stuff*, he settled for ruffling his son's hair instead.

The basketball looked like a beach ball in the five-year-old's pudgy hands. Yet he was growing, Matthew realized. Like the crocuses and jonquils shooting up in the flower beds along the south side of the house, Joey was sprouting taller every day. He was changing fast. Too fast and too often without his father there to see the changes. Matthew was missing things. Too many things.

Fighting to keep his sense of loss from undercutting their backyard fun, Matthew ordered himself to count his wins, not his losses. All things considered, it could be worse. After his wife had died and her parents had petitioned for and won custody of Joey, he'd thought he'd never see his son again. The Handcocks had that kind of power. Settling for every-other-weekend visits had been grating, but better than nothing.

All that was about to change, though. He was tired of waiting to have Joey with him permanently. He'd been working toward that end when he'd bought his house three years earlier. It was a nice neighborhood, quiet streets, green grass, a park a few blocks away. It had everything a boy would need to grow up healthy and happy.

Soon. Very soon, he promised Joey silently. *I'm going to have you back with me permanently. Back where you belong.*

"Try again, bud," he said, shaking off the grim reality of the past by focusing on the future. "This time you'll make one."

He hid a grin as Joey shuffled his feet, double-palmed several enthusiastic dribbles, and snuck a determined glance at the hoop mounted on the garage.

Joey's failed attempt and grumbled "Shoot!" went

right over Matthew's head, though, when a loud crash shattered the lazy afternoon quiet.

Jerking his head toward the adjoining backyard, he cocked an ear and listened. All he heard in the aftermath was Chubby Checker twisting again on the radio in the garage. But he knew.

"Gee, Dad. What was that?"

Matthew propped his hands on his hips and studied the driveway beneath his feet. "I'll give you two guesses."

Joey squished his freckled face into a puzzled frown before comprehension dawned. "Katie?"

"You got it. What do you suppose she's gotten herself into this time?"

Joey, the budding hero since they'd saved Katie from her toe-eating bathtub on his last visit, grabbed his basketball and tucked it under his arm. "We'd better go find out. She probably needs us again."

Why me? Matthew asked the sky as he followed Joey across the yard. He thought longingly of the Browns. Until a month earlier, when they'd resettled in Florida, the elderly couple had been his neighbors to the south.

They'd been good neighbors. Quiet, orderly neighbors. He missed them. Missed the friendly waves across the driveway, missed Dora's oatmeal raisin cookies and motherly smiles. Missed seeing John puttering with his lawn mower and listening to the occasional fish story over the hedge.

He missed the *normalcy* of it all. His new neighbor

wouldn't recognize normal if it snuck up and bit her on her saucy little tush.

He hadn't had a moment of pure R & R since Katie-the-walking-disaster McDonald had infiltrated the block. Her misadventures had kept him busier than an elf at Christmas and her short shorts were playing ten kinds of havoc with his peace of mind.

The woman didn't have a gram of common sense rattling around in that stubborn blond head of hers. She'd never heard of the word "limitation" and honestly thought that no matter what needed doing, she could do it. Like the day he'd caught her lugging a fifteen-foot metal extension ladder from her garage to the house. In all probability, it weighed more than she did. In all probability, it had more gray matter, too, he'd thought grumpily as he'd watched her struggle.

For all of ten seconds he'd debated. It had taken another ten to sprint out his back door and wrestle the ladder away from her. It had taken the rest of the afternoon, however, to clean out her eaves.

She'd fed him homemade cookies and lemonade as payment. He'd wolfed the cookies down and felt guilty for comparing them favorably to Dora's.

The times that he'd saved her from herself since were too numerous to count. And now it looked like he was about to play the reluctant rescuer again, when all he wanted to do was keep his distance.

Yet when he walked into her garage and spotted

her, he felt that special warmth she kindled heat up and spread like summer sunshine through his chest. The grin came automatically now.

"I did *not* call you, Spencer," she said tartly when she caught a glimpse of his shadow on the garage floor. "And I do *not* need you. So you can just trot back over to your own yard and entertain yourself."

This from the lady sprawled across the rafters of her garage. She put him in mind of a kite that had crashed into the limbs of a tree.

She had grease on her nose, a wrench in her hand, and a look of belligerent determination etched across a face he looked forward to seeing far more often than was prudent.

He crossed his arms over his chest and leaned a shoulder against the door frame. "Why would we want to go back over there when the seats are so cheap here and the show is so much better?"

She flashed him a fake smile. For Joey she produced a real one. "Joey, please send your father home. *You* can stay, though, if you want to."

Joey craned his neck to look up at her. "What'er ya doin', Katie?"

"Yeah, Katie," Matthew said. "What'er ya doin'?"

She fielded his smug grin with a disgruntled smirk. "I'm installing a garage door opener and I'm *doin'* just fine, thank you very much."

"Ah. So you *planned* on the ladder tipping over and

stranding you fifteen feet above a cement floor. You straddle that rafter very well, by the way."

She glared at him. "And you have a nasty knack for catching me at my worst. I've got to tell you, Ace, it's really beginning to annoy me."

Due to the unfortunate—or fortunate—placement of his kitchen window, Matthew had caught her at her best too. While he left for the construction site or for his office most mornings before she did, he was often home when she pulled in at night. The first time she'd zipped into her drive and slipped out of her little compact, he'd had to look twice to make sure it was her. The transformation from Calamity Katie to Career Woman Kate was nothing short of phenomenal.

He was particularly partial to the stern little bun thing she sometimes tortured her hair into, and the tailored gray business suit she usually wore when she was in her career-matron mode. Sedate and regal, she looked the part of a corporate killer, with her briefcase tucked under her arm and her three-inch pumps. He liked the looks of her even better, though, when she wore her hair down and her clothes were loose and flowing. She really did have great legs and she wasn't afraid to show them off with a deep slit or a brief hem of a skirt.

Those glimpses of her quintessential woman persona, however, were fleeting. As soon as she got home, she'd disappear into her house, duck into the closest phone booth, and reappear in her off-duty uniform: short shorts and soft clingy T-shirts that were as bright and cheerful as the flowers she'd planted along the side of her house.

The rest of the evening she'd charge around the yard on her quest of the night, which could be anything from gardening, to oil changing, to a little extracurricular rewiring, and all were efforts at driving him nuts. In short, she became the walking disaster he'd grown to know and love . . . figuratively speaking, of course. Love would never be an issue.

Neither would lust, he reminded himself staunchly. The very first day they'd met, they'd both drawn lines that neither of them intended to cross. At some unspoken level, they'd acknowledged that no matter how high the voltage skittering between them got, "neighborly" was as close to intimacy as they were ever going to get. Since then, they'd worked hard at maintaining that distance.

He still didn't know her reasons for needing that distance, but he wasn't about to lose sight of his. Joey, tugging impatiently on the frayed leg of his cutoffs, was a constant and welcome reminder.

"Are we going to get her down, Dad?"

"Oh, I don't know," he said, considering Katie as if she were some scrap lumber that might or might not come in handy some day. "Maybe we should just leave her up there. At least we'll know where she is."

She glanced at Joey to make sure he couldn't see her left hand, then she flashed Matthew a digital expression that was universally interpreted as a suggestion to take his attitude and put it where the sun don't shine. He countered with a raised eyebrow and his own sign for "Shame on you," knowing as he did that his grin grossly diminished the scolding.

It had become a game between them, lots of good-natured grousing and innocuous teasing. She was very good at it, and he appreciated the enthusiasm with which she played. She made it easy for him to keep his distance and yet enjoy her. He only wished he didn't enjoy her quite so much.

Just then she snarled something under her breath, and the wrench she'd been wielding clattered noisily to the garage floor.

Matthew looked down at the wrench, which had landed by his feet, then back up at her. "I guess it's lucky for me you've got a lousy aim."

She blew a tangled lock of sunflower-blonde hair away from her face and eyed him stonily. "If I'd been aiming at you, Spencer, you wouldn't still be standing there to talk about it."

He chuckled. "Getting a little testy, aren't we?"

"Getting a little too pompous for our blue jeans, aren't we? Gloating does not become you, Ace. Let's just get it over with, okay?"

He pushed away from the door and ambled toward

the fallen ladder. "Are you suggesting that you actually could use a little help?"

"Gosh, you're awfully cute and you really do have nice buns, but it does not excuse you for being such an overbearing male supremacist slug." She smiled sweetly. "Now, it kills me to have to ask, but would you *please* be so kind as to help me down from here?"

"Well, since you asked so nice, it'll be our pleasure, won't it, Joey?"

Joey giggled. He didn't have the slightest notion of what was going on between his father and Katie. He only knew that whatever it was, Katie made his dad laugh. That was enough for him.

It was more than enough for Katie. More than enough of what, she wasn't altogether sure. She only knew that if she could keep Matthew from taking her seriously, then they wouldn't have to deal with this male/female intensity nonsense that insisted on sneaking up on her. And, if she wasn't mistaken, it snuck up on him too.

She really didn't understand it. Men had never taken her seriously, so it shouldn't have been that difficult to add Matthew to the fold. She knew what men saw at first glance—a long, rangy blond, cute and thin, with nice legs and a marginal chest, but too flighty and enamored with cause and purpose to be worth the trouble of a second glance. One guy had gone so far as to inform her on his way out the door that he preferred a soft, submissive woman, not a Dorothy-do-gooder who was as independent as a wildcat oil rigger and as maniacally fearless as Mel Gibson in *Lethal Weapon*. Another had told her he found her electric blue eyes hard to meet, let alone hold.

Matthew seemed to have no such problem. Every time they got within eye contact of each other, the air heated by several degrees. In fact, all of his reactions—reactions she was sure he was fighting—were different.

That was why she had to get away from him. Him and his sexy brown eyes and deep tan, not to mention his teasing smile that hinted at a seduction she suspected the man wasn't even aware he was suggesting.

She didn't know how much longer she could keep up her own pretense of indifference. It was getting increasingly harder to play the roll of Nellie the nutty neighbor. Although, truth to tell, she really hadn't had to work all that hard at perpetuating that image. Things—*ridiculous things*—just seemed to happen whenever Matthew came within snickering distance.

And "distance," she knew, was the key word. For the past seven of her twenty-eight years, distance was the only thing she'd really wanted from a man. She'd gotten too close once, believed in someone once, and she'd been hurt. Who needed it? It wasn't worth the hassle. Especially when she knew that for her, involvement with any man could never be anything more than short-term.

With a man like Matthew, though, distance was an increasingly hard thing to keep.

Lucky for her, he was fighting the attraction as aggressively as she was. She'd caught enough glimpses into his character over the past two weeks to know he was a good, solid, dependable man. She was the antithesis of his solidity and, she sensed, the last thing he needed in his life. For his sake as well as her own, it wouldn't do to let him know the extent of his effect on her. To achieve that end, she couldn't show any weakness.

She watched as he reset the ladder beneath her and steadied it. "So," she said, "I suppose this means I owe you—again."

"You can consider the bill paid in full," he began, then stopped and cleared his throat as his gaze traveled the length of her legs, "if you'll shimmy on down here and let me finish the job you started."

Painfully aware of the brevity of her shorts and that he was watching her every move, she shifted and slid until her feet hit the top of the ladder.

"Do you have to stand right there?" she asked, all huffy indignation when he planted a hand on either side of the ladder directly beneath her.

"I do. With your track record, I don't trust you more than three feet off the ground."

She didn't trust herself within three inches of him, which was exactly where she was going to land if she descended into the circle his arms created. His bare arms. And bare chest. Broad, tanned, sexy bare chest. Oh, boy.

It was clear, though, from the look in his eyes that he wasn't about to budge.

Okay, if he could handle it, so could she.

Setting her jaw, she presented her tush and scaled the rungs like a professional roofer until she hit the last one. That one was the killer. She stumbled and would have hit the floor hard if he hadn't caught her.

The hand on her arm held firm yet gentle. The hand on her hip settled tight and low, and after its initial steadying, hot and intimate. When he turned her to face him, the look in his eyes was just too hot for the May afternoon. She felt the heat clear down to her toes, with a few distressing detours along the way.

It was a July look. A real scorcher that was a sultry and not so subtle suggestion of midnight thunder and summer lightning and the magic two people could make in one bed.

Though his grip on her arm loosened, he continued to hold her . . . a little longer than necessary, a little closer than wise.

"You okay?" he finally asked.

Okay? No, she wasn't okay. She was, however, determined to douse the heat sizzling between them.

And she'd chew on her wrench before she'd admit she didn't need a shaky ladder to knock her off her feet. His scent alone, spring sunshine and backyard sweat, could have done it. The dark, dusky look in his eyes could have done it. It still might, she realized as his gaze dropped to her mouth and she felt her knees weaken. It not only might, it would—soon—if she didn't do something to diffuse the situation.

"Honestly," she muttered, pulling away and dusting her hands on the seat of her shorts. "You men. You're all alike. Those macho hormones stand right to attention the minute they suspect a female is in over her head."

Too late, after a glance at the fly of his cutoffs, she realized his physical condition matched her unfortunate choice of analogies. The old joke formed in her mind before she could squelch it: *Is that a flashlight in your pocket or are you just glad to see me?*

Fighting a hysterical laugh—it had to be hysterics, because this certainly wasn't a laughing matter—she tried to gloss over her remark with a wisecrack.

"Down, boy." Oh, Lord. Would someone please stuff something in her mouth? she begged silently.

Taking a deep breath, she met his laughing eyes without flinching and tried for indignant. "You don't think I can get it up by myself, do you?"

Stee-rike three.

There were homes for people like her, Katie thought.

She wished she were in one right now. A room with a view beyond the bars on the windows would be nice. And a pool. She'd really like a pool.

"Are we still talking about the garage door opener?" he asked, smiling at her with an irritating combination of mischief and little-boy innocence.

It was the mischief that got her dander back up. "Well, we're not talking about . . ." Her voice trailed off as her eyes betrayed her by darting back to that damn fly. ". . . flashlights," she finished lamely, and wished she'd never learned to talk.

If he hadn't made a stab at toning down his grin, she might have picked up her wrench and showed him just how good her aim was. At this range she was sure she could teach him a thing or two about what happened to people who had too much fun at her expense.

"Oh, you can do it, all right," he teased. Reading the warning glare in her eyes, he added in an all-business tone, "Get the garage door opener up, that is. It's just that your methods make me a little nervous."

Her methods made *him* nervous? Although retreat was the coward's way out, survival was still her top priority. She'd see about having the yellow stripe removed from her back tomorrow. Today she was going to run like hell before she made an even bigger fool of herself.

"It's only because I'm almost done and because I could use some help making lemonade that I'm going to agree to letting you finish the job. How about it, Joey?" She turned to the boy. "You look like you've got a good set of muscles there. Up for squeezing the sour out of a few lemons while your dad plays out his handyman fantasies?"

Joey screwed up his face comically. "I thought lemonade came in a can."

Back in her stride, she threw Matthew a look that suggested he'd sadly neglected his son's education. "And I suppose you think milk is made in plastic cartons," she said, looking back at Joey.

She got the giggle she'd been fishing for.

"No, silly. Milk comes from cows."

"Cows?" she repeated, feigning surprise as she shepherded Joey toward the house and out of touching distance of all that bare skin, out of striking distance of those eyes. "Milk comes from cows? I think maybe you'd better fill me in."

An hour later Katie knew that squeezing a few lemons and distracting herself with Joey weren't enough to do the trick. No, she had to lend more credibility to her pretense of not being affected by Matthew. So she asked him and his son to dinner that night. After all, she told herself, she owed Matthew for finishing the work on the garage door opener for her. Besides, that's what neighbors did. They acted neighborly. And Joey, in addition to being a delightful little boy, would provide an excellent buffer.

In retrospect, she realized she should have known she couldn't count on a five-year-old past nine o'clock. After the burgers, he wore himself out chasing lightning bugs. He fought it every nod of the way, but he was no match for the sandman.

And she, after a busy day and half a bottle of wine, proved to be no match for the mood that the man and the moon created.

THREE

The night was like one of those special spring evenings Katie remembered from back home on the farm downstate. The moon hung high and round and glowed a pale lemon yellow. Since sunset the hedge along the property line had come alive with the calming cadence of little night creatures. In the background, KCMO played on and on. Sultry and slow, the dreamy lyrics and melody of the Eagles' "Peaceful Easy Feeling" blended in perfect harmony with nature's chorus.

Her deck was just big enough to comfortably hold a pair of cushioned deck chairs, a chaise, her grill, and a small, round glass-topped table. It was backyard suburbia at its generic best, and deviated from the norm only because of her special affection for flowering plants. The bougainvillea was her favorite, although the ivy geraniums ran a close second. The wealth of floral scents embellished the lazy music, both natural and man-made, that surrounded then.

Joey, his jar of fireflies still clutched in his small fist, made a soft, sleeping child sound and curled into himself on the chaise. A blanket she'd snagged from her linen closet hugged his little body and warded off the light chill of the still May night.

Matthew, as relaxed as she'd ever seen him, slouched in a loose-limbed sprawl in the chair across from hers, a half-full wineglass balanced lazily on his thigh.

He'd been quiet the past several minutes, deep in thought, his head back as he stared at the stars. She'd have thought he was asleep except for the occasional stab he made at playing footsie with her size sevens, which were propped opposite his on the table between them.

Somehow, it had gotten to be ten o'clock, and she knew they should have called it a night long ago. Somehow, neither of them seemed to want to end it. Somehow, she had to figure out a way to do just that.

She felt too comfortable with him, too cozy and too weary of tamping down the flames that kept flaring up between them.

She knew of only one sure way to kill them.

"So," she began, all casual indifference, "your lady is very pretty."

It took a moment for him to react. When he did, it

was with a subtle shifting of his shoulders and a slow lifting of his glass to his lips.

Katie's reactions were nowhere near as passive as his. Ten kinds of feelings ricocheted around inside her at the mention of the woman in Matthew's life. None of them were benevolent. With great difficulty she managed to keep from squirming in her chair. Her heart, however, had launched into a tango as she battled a jealousy she hated herself for feeling.

She'd seen the petite, sophisticated brunette come calling on more than one occasion during the past two weeks. Shameless, Katie had watched from her kitchen window as a sedate sedan pulled up Matthew's drive and the woman opened his door as if she had every right to be there. Clearly, she did have that right, if the greetings Matthew gave her were any indication. His sexy smile would welcome her, his large hand would settle possessively at the small of her back, and the kiss he would drop on her perfectly sculptured cheek spoke of familiarity and commitment.

"I'd like you to meet her sometime," he said at last in that low, steady voice that always managed to set her senses humming. "I think you'd like her."

She didn't think anything of the sort. "I'm sure I would."

"She's good for me," he added after a long silence and in a tone she chose not to interpret as an attempt to convince himself as well as her. "And she's good for Joey."

"That's good. Good," she repeated, and fortified herself with a little wine. Then a little more. "He's a very special little boy."

She watched Matthew's dark gaze shift from the sky to his sleeping son. His expression transformed from a look of lazy contentment to one of intense private pain. On a blinding flash of insight, she recognized that pain. It was a helpless, gnawing ache, a vital, living entity that wouldn't let go. She'd been bearing it herself for several years. What she didn't know—what she suddenly needed to know—was what was causing it in Matthew. She hurt for him and could no more stop her next question than she could stop breathing.

"Where's Joey's mother?" Even as she asked, a part of her was wary of the answer.

His gaze cut to hers through the darkness. In that suspended moment she was certain he was going to tell her to mind her own business. In the next, however, she wanted to jump out of her chair, wrap him in her arms, and make his pain go away. Only she knew from experience it would never be that easy.

"That was incredibly rude," she said quickly. "I'm sorry, Matthew. It's none of my business. I . . . shouldn't have asked."

"It's all right," he said as he leaned forward and poured them both more wine. "Carol died just before

Joey's first birthday. Cancer," he added flatly as he settled back and contemplated his glass.

She pinched her eyes shut and cursed herself for her insensitivity. "I'm sorry," she said finally. To say more would minimize the sorrow she felt for all he must have gone through.

"Yeah. We all were. She was a very special woman."

"And you loved her very much."

He tipped up his glass and took a deep swallow. "Yes."

She watched his throat work and damned herself for opening up a wound that was obviously still in the healing process.

"Losing her pretty well ripped me apart."

Katie knew all about losing. Once upon a time, she'd lost someone too. A loss she could have prevented. A pain no one should have suffered. Matthew's soft voice brought her back to the present, and suddenly she didn't know if she was strong enough to hear what he seemed on the verge of telling her.

"I lost my grip on everything for a while afterward . . . everything but a bottle of bourbon. My business was the first to go."

From their backyard conversations and his penchant for fixing whatever he'd decided she couldn't fix, she knew he owned his own construction business. He built mostly low-income homes and apartments, he'd told her with an almost imperceptible trace of pride in his tone. Now and then he picked up a bigger contract for an individual who was tired of the condo scene and wanted an original and well-crafted home. He kept a crew of ten busy and his books in the black. She was surprised to hear it hadn't always been that way.

What he said next surprised her even more, but clarified the depth of the anguish he was feeling.

"And then I lost Joey too."

Her own grief, which she'd allowed too close to the surface, ran in tandem. *And then I lost Carrie too*. It was a not so distant echo that got tangled for a moment with his. With great effort she separated herself from her memories, held her silence, and listened.

"Carol's parents sued for custody and won."

The hurt she felt for both him and Joey filled her chest and then her eyes. She watched the hard set of his jaw through the threatening tears.

In the moonlight, in the silence, she knew the moment he saw them. "It's not as bad as it sounds, Katie. The Handcocks are nice people. In the beginning, yes, they didn't approve of me when Carol and I became involved. I'm strictly middle-class, blue-collar, white bread. They're upper-crust-society rich. But they saw how much I loved her and they did the right thing and accepted our marriage. They saw, too, after I lost her that what I was doing to myself and to Joey was no good."

"But to take him away from you—"

"Was the best and the only thing they could have done," he interrupted gently. "The way I was acting during that time left the court little choice but to grant their petition. Initially I had difficulty—to put it mildly—accepting that they'd done it out of love and with Joey's best interests in mind."

All that explained why she'd only seen Joey at the house every other weekend. It didn't mean she had to like it. "A boy should be with his father," she said.

The vehemence of her statement earned her a smile. "Down, Katie. He will be. It took me almost a year to wake up and admit that booze wasn't the answer. It took another two to bring the business back around. When I did, the Handcocks were right there, ready to agree to less-restricted visitation rights. They've been very generous on that count, considering they have the kind of power and connections to make sure I'd never see him again. But they didn't do that. They've been supportive, if stern, in letting me know that when I get my life back together and can provide Joey with a solid, stable home life, they'll consider returning custody to me."

"So what's the holdup?" she asked, still in a bit of a pique. "It's obvious to anyone with eyes that you love that child. You're too healthy and too together to be a problem drinker. Your business is successful again." She stopped, exasperated on his behalf, even miffed with him because he had a choice. A choice was something she'd never had. He could be fighting harder. "What more do they want?"

His silence told her he was having difficulty forming an answer to her question.

After a long moment of searching his face, she figured it out for herself. To an extent, her conclusion disgusted her. But she saw the sense in it and knew that if she were in his shoes, she'd do anything and everything to get her child back.

"I see," she said. "The Handcocks want *all* the pieces put together, a *complete* home to send Joey back to. Papa Bear, Baby Bear, and Momma Bear. And now that you've met Ms. Right—Lisa was handpicked by the Handcocks, I take it?" When he didn't dispute her deduction, she continued, hating herself when she heard the accusatory edge in her tone, "—you're one step away from having Joey with you full-time."

The implication left her cold. So did the look in his eyes.

"Joey needs a complete family," he said, matter-of-factly. "Lisa can help me provide that for him."

And what can Lisa provide for you? she wanted to ask. Was there love, or convenience? Passion or peace of mind? It wasn't any of her business. It shouldn't matter to her, yet it did. Far too much. And aside from the fact that she was devastatingly attracted to him, she didn't have the foggiest notion why. She'd learned long ago that she was not marriage or mother material.

"So," she said with false brightness, "it's wedding bells in the not so distant future?"

His gaze met hers for a long moment before it drifted back to the night sky. "We haven't exactly gotten to the date-setting stage yet, but . . ." He hesitated, then took another sip of his wine. "Yeah, maybe. It seems to be the next logical step in the course of things."

Logical, she repeated silently. Matthew and *Star Trek*'s unemotional Mr. Spock birds of a feather? She thought not. Spock was incapable of feeling. Matthew was incapable of *not* feeling. He radiated love and compassion every time he looked with such hungry longing at his son. She thought it noble and yet very sad that to obtain his goal of full-time fatherhood, he might be sacrificing his own needs to ensure he wouldn't compromise Joey's. But they were his choices to make and they weren't hers to judge. She'd like better for him, that was all. He deserved honest passion and undying love. The kind she could give him.

And that's enough of that, McDonald, she warned herself, and tossed back another swallow of wine.

"What about Katie McDonald?" she heard him ask through a haze of weary acceptance and far too much disappointment.

Cradling her wineglass in her hands, she stared down into its glistening contents. "What about her?"

"I've basically told you my life story. It's only fair that I hear yours. Other than the fact that you migrated north from farm country and that you have a habit of getting yourself into jams, I don't really know much about you."

And he never would, she thought. She considered how much to tell him to satisfy his curiosity and not compromise the past she protected. "What do you want to know?"

"For starters, what deep dark secrets you might be hiding."

He was only half teasing. She could hear it in his tone, see it in his eyes. He really wanted to know. Wanted her to share her life the way he'd shared his. He deserved that from her. And she was tempted to tell him that she, too, knew what it felt like to lose someone she loved. Someone small and special whom she'd never been granted the chance to know.

She was tempted, but not willing to expose the raw edges of that particular pain. Not even to him. So she hedged. Something she had buckets of practice doing.

"Secrets?" she asked, affecting a lightness she didn't feel. "Come on, Spencer. Does this look like a face that could keep a secret?"

Matthew stared in pensive silence at the face in question. Once he would have said no, there were no secrets there. Now he wasn't so sure. That night, and other times when he'd caught her watching Joey with a wistfulness that brought a sharp sting to his eyes, he'd thought he'd sensed a secret or two. A hidden pain. A fierce longing. Whatever those looks meant, she had definitely managed to keep the cause to herself.

One thing, though, she hadn't been able to hide was her feelings for him. More often than not, her thoughts were as clear as the sky backlighting the full moon. She was falling in love with him, and, if he wasn't mistaken, she was falling in love with Joey too.

Dammit, Katie, he swore tiredly to himself. Why did she have to charge into his neighborhood, into his life, and complicate everything? And why was it so easy for him to let her?

She'd just folded and tucked his relationship with Lisa into a stark, sterile box with a plain brown wrapper. Her silent accusation should have irritated him, but the way she'd laid it out, he supposed he did sound cold and calculated. To an extent, he guessed he was. The end, however—having Joey back with him—justified everything.

So why was he feeling so hollow inside?

It wasn't as if he didn't care about Lisa. He liked and respected her. Those feelings, he knew, were mutual and mutually satisfactory. Like him, Lisa had lost the one great love in her life. And like him, she had no expectations of ever finding that kind of love again.

What they had together made sense: friendship, affection, trust. It was a sturdier base to found a marriage on than those of many of his friends. And the bottom line, as Katie had guessed, was that the Handcocks approved. Lisa would be a solid, dependable influence in Joey's life.

He sighed. He didn't need to defend his motives to anyone. And how Katie felt about what he did shouldn't matter. Yet he knew it did.

He glanced over at her silhouette. After a long moment he forced himself to look away. Just play the game, he ordered himself. Just play the game like you have been most days since you met her. The stakes were too high to change tactics now.

Yet after all those valid arguments, he couldn't help but probe further. "If there are no secrets, Katie, then what are the plans?" Damning himself even as he posed the question, he tried to cover with a not so solid attempt at teasing. "I mean, what makes Katie tick? Explain again, if you would be so kind, what the hell it is you do? I'm still a little lost on that one."

Katie picked right up on her cue to play the part of the nettled feminist. Settling back in her chair, she said loftily, "I like to think of myself as a self-styled female Ralph Nader."

He chuckled and fell with ease into his designated role of pest and tormentor, knowing it would make them both more comfortable. "Never in a million years,

Katie, sweet, would I put you and Ralph Nader in the same profession. Besides"—he waggled his brows suggestively—"you've got it all over him in the legs department."

"Typical male reaction," she said, rising to his bait just as he'd known she would. "You don't bother to compare professional ability, you just shoot right for the physical comparisons. 'If it wears a bra,'" she went on, affecting the image of a cigar-smoking, belly-bulging chairman-of-the-board bigot, "'and if it can't stand up to go to the bathroom, it couldn't possibly be capable of competing in the real world.'"

He barked out a surprised laugh, first at her outrageous sense of humor, then at the idea of her in a bra. To date, he'd never seen her wear one. No doubt that was part of his problem.

"You are such a naughty girl," he said, "but you've made your point with a very sharp pencil. Please consider an apology extended for my thinking with my *typical male hormones* instead of with my head. And for the record, the question of your capability has never been an issue in my book. It's more a question of why you do what you do."

"If you don't question my abilities," she asked, sidestepping the question of motivation, "why is it that every time I turn around, you're hauling me off a ladder or jerking a wrench out of my hand?"

She had a point there. He knew the answer to that

one, but decided to keep it to himself for both their sakes. He rushed over to save her not from herself but because of his own inability to resist playing out his white knight fantasy. She prompted that reaction in him. He just couldn't help himself. Neither could he admit it to her.

"I haul you off ladders and out from under cars . . ." He had to stop and regroup when a vividly erotic picture came to mind of a pair of long, superior legs stretched out from under the belly of her car, followed by another of her descending that shaky ladder. He shifted uncomfortably in his chair as something other than his head reacted with a swift and sudden thickening.

"I'm waiting," she singsonged, grinning.

"I haul you off ladders," he began again, managing to react to her tone, not the memory, "because I'm better at fixing things than fixing bodies. I don't do first aid, Katie. It's basic instinct for me to figure out how to stop a potential blood flow before it ever starts."

"My guess is that you just like to show off."

"Well, there is that," he conceded with one of those smiles she managed to win so easily. "Look, I understand your need to be independent, but sometimes certain projects merit calling in the professionals."

"You're treading on thin ice again."

"A garage door opener, Katie? Come on. That's a

job for a carpenter, not a . . . a . . . What are you again, anyway?"

Even in the dark, he could tell she wanted to slug him. Distance kept her from it. Distance and a laziness brought on by the wine and the music and the moonlight.

"Consumer advocate," she stated slowly and distinctly. "Now say it with me, boys and girls."

When he just grinned again, she continued. "And if the directions on the box say that anyone can do it, it's my job to see if what they promise is true."

"So what you're telling me is that you risk life, not to mention a fine set of limbs"—he heard her soft growl and smiled—"to find out for the American consumer if it's fact or fantasy when a product makes such a claim."

"My," she said, sounding impressed. "He not only walks and talks, he's capable of analytical thought. And here I thought you were just another pretty face."

"I'll ignore the sarcasm because I know you can't help yourself. But at least be honest, Katie. Some of the stunts you pull are downright dangerous."

"Okay. I admit that I push it sometimes, but for the most part, my job can be pretty boring. Occasionally I need a little diversion."

"Why don't you just tell me about the boring parts so I can sleep better tonight."

"You want boring? I'll give you boring. Most of what I do is research and write articles for *Today's*

Market magazine on best consumer buys, consumer fraud, advice on what to watch out for."

His loud, affected snore brought the laugh he wanted and a not so gentle nudge from her foot.

"Sometimes, though," she continued, "I start out with boring and end up with an in-depth investigation that gets a little spicy."

He opened one eye. "You weren't paying attention. *Spicy* is the kind of stuff I *don't* want to hear about."

"Like the time I exposed a bogus insurance scam that preyed on senior citizens," she went on, ignoring him.

"I definitely don't want to hear about this."

"These guys were real vultures. They'd go door to door at senior citizen's apartment complexes and use scare tactics to convince the residents that their perfectly adequate health insurance coverage wasn't enough to pay the bills if they had a lengthy illness. Before they left, they'd have those poor people frightened into buying these worthless policies for outrageously inflated premiums."

In spite of his protest, her story intrigued and incensed him every bit as much as it did her. "Pure sleaze."

"You got that right. Anyway, I helped shut down their operation. It was that particular investigation that landed me the position at *Today's Market*. It also earned me a few threats to back off."

His heart slammed against his chest like a guard dog against a chain link fence. "You were threatened?" he asked, straightening slowly.

She nodded. "Threats, they soon learned, were the last thing that would work with me."

He wanted to shake her for her recklessness before he locked her in a padded room somewhere where she couldn't go out and hurt herself. Curbing that explosive instinct, he forced himself to praise her instead for the good she'd done. Then he calmly issued some brotherly advice. "You've got to be careful, Katie. Those guys may have been all bluff, but someday you'll run into someone who isn't."

The look she gave him set all his senses on edge. Her next question nearly sent him into shock.

"You're a building contractor," she said. "What do you know about Jim Brackman?"

He narrowed his eyes, meeting her determined gaze, and sat up straight in his chair. "You're *not* messing around in Brackman's business." He drilled her with a look that should have made her quiver. Katie, he was learning fast, never did what what she was supposed to do.

"What do you know about him?" she repeated, unflinching.

He set down his glass and scrubbed a hand over his jaw. "I know that if Brackman Electric bids on a contract I'm looking into, I pull out."

"Why?"

"Let's just say I prefer not to be involved in any projects with him."

"In other words, he's as crooked as a corkscrew."

"No other words are necessary," he said darkly. "Those say it just fine."

"So, our tip is accurate," she mused aloud. "He uses inferior materials and cuts corners to pad his profit."

He leaned in closer, making sure he had her attention. "Katie, don't go poking around in Brackman's business. Please trust me on this one."

Her eyes took on an intensity that was unmistakable even in the night shadows. "The man works in your field. Surely you'd like to see him exposed."

Matthew sighed deeply. "There's an old seventies song about not tugging on Superman's cape and *not* messing around with Jim. Jim Brackman could've been the man Croce had in mind when he wrote that song." Matthew was dead serious and wanted her to know it. "If you haven't gotten into this issue yet, don't. If you have, back off."

She smiled, but he knew he had her attention. "Don't you think you're overreacting?"

"Overreacting my ass. Katie, I'm telling you, you *don't* want to make this man your enemy."

"What I *don't* want is to see any more housing projects built with inferior wiring. The potential for fire is monumental. Think of the lives that might be at stake. If I can do something to prevent disaster, then I'm going to do it. Brackman may not have a conscience, but I do. Knowing what I know, I *can't* leave it alone. That would be as criminal as his actions. Excuse me, his *alleged* actions. Besides, if I handle the investigation right, it will be all over except the shouting before he knows he's been found out."

Matthew could see there was no stopping her. He could also see that he'd best take his own advice and let her mind her own business.

This insight into the chances she was willing to take for her career reinforced his original argument for keeping his distance. He'd already known he couldn't afford to get involved with her. The risks she took were just too . . . risky. Even without this latest revelation, he doubted the Handcocks would approve of her. She was too much of a free spirit, too Bohemian, too . . . He stopped short. Since when had he been toying with the idea of introducing her to Joey's grandparents? he asked himself in disgust.

What disgusted him even more, though, was the thought that he felt he needed their approval for anything. Whose life was he leading here, anyway?

"Ummm, I haven't heard that one in a long time."

Her dreamy tone brought him back to the moment and the song. The haunting strains from "Theme from *A Summer Place*" drifted into the night.

"Percy Faith, 1960," he said automatically, even though the turn of his thoughts still plagued him.

"Hey, you're pretty good." She sounded pleased and surprised. And superior. "You're off a year, though. It was '59."

"'60," he insisted, then added distractedly, "February, to be exact, number one for nine weeks."

She swirled what was left of her wine in her glass and eyed him with renewed interest. "I guess I ought to be impressed. I would be, too, if you were right. But, my dear Mr. Wolf-Man-Jack-you-ain't, the year was nineteen hundred and fifty-nine."

He gave her a patronizing smile, glad for the diversion from his unsettling conclusions. "Look, McDonald, you're messing with the wrong guy here. Don't even *think* that you can out-top-forty me."

"Oooo, do I detect a hint in challenge in there somewhere?" In the moonlight, her eyes took on a sheen of excitement as she sat up straighter. She looked pretty and alive. And desirable.

Pretending to ignore all three descriptions, he downed the last of his wine. "I don't take candy from babies and I don't make wagers with amateurs."

"And he's modest too."

"Okay, hotshot, try me." He kicked back again, getting comfortable. "*Then* decide if I know of which I speak."

She tossed several titles at him. Without missing a

beat, he supplied the names of the artists, the year of release, and the top number each song had hit on the charts.

"That was your best shot?" he asked, patting back a ho-hum yawn.

"So how come you know all the oldies so well? It wasn't exactly your generation."

He grinned when he saw her begrudging but sexy pout. "It wasn't yours either, sweet cheeks, but that didn't stop you from falling in love with the music."

"It is great, isn't it?"

"Katie," he said, suddenly serious. Suddenly compelled by her wistful, dreamy look to stop with the trivia and find out some answers. Suddenly out of his ever-loving mind. "Why aren't you involved with someone?"

"Involved?" she echoed after a lengthy silence that told him she was as startled as he by his change of tack.

"Involved," he repeated, hearing too much interest in his voice. "You know, love, relationship, romance?"

She was quiet again for so long, he thought she wasn't going to answer. He was already wishing he hadn't asked. When she finally shrugged and gathered herself, he almost told her to never mind. Almost.

"I guess I quit believing in romance a long time ago."

He stared at her, seeing her struggle to hide the pain. So, she'd been hurt. He'd figured as much. It wasn't a phenomenon exclusive to her. It happened to almost everyone at one time or another. She was young. Vulnerable. She was beautiful and desirable. And if what he knew of her so far was any indicator, she was also resilient. "You're too young to sound so jaded," he said.

Avoiding his eyes, she picked absently at the hem of her shorts. "Let's just say I don't do well with relationships."

"I find that hard to believe. As a matter of fact, I can see you as a major contributor in a relationship."

"Well, there you go," she said, trying to affect that flip attitude of hers. "Once again, that shows how much you know. My job keeps me so involved, I don't have it left in me to contribute." She shook her head. "Nope. Commitment is too messy. Too complicated."

She was the one who was complicated, he thought. And to top it off, she was complicating the hell out of his life at this very moment. "What about sex?" he asked before he could stop himself.

Startled, she met his eyes, then looked away. "Overrated."

He smiled and thought of all the ways he could convince her otherwise. About how much fun it would be to convince her otherwise. About how badly he *wanted* to convince otherwise.

"What about babies?" he asked, not stopping to

question why he didn't just back off. When he met those telling eyes of hers, he could have kicked himself. Pain, sharp and cutting, flashed like a blade before she lowered her lashes and shook her head.

"Let's do a little reality check here, Ace," she said. "To quote you and your insightful wisdom, I can hardly take care of myself, let alone take care of a baby. I mean, can you really see me in the role?"

He saw the way Joey came alive whenever she was around. Saw the way she'd lit up like a sunrise the first time he'd thrown his little arms around her and clambered up onto her lap. And he'd seen the look in her eyes that night when she'd covered him with her blanket and made sure he was warm and comfortable. "Yeah," he said so softly, it was barely a whisper between them. "I can see you in the role just fine."

He could see her other roles too. Lover. Wife. Both were roles he was having more and more difficulty imagining filled by anyone else.

She was right. A reality check was definitely in order.

Many more of those looks, many more of these feelings, and he was going to make many, many errors in judgment. Errors that might be irreversible and impossible to live with.

Joey stirred and mumbled, "Catch it, Dad," in his sleep.

Across the moonlight-dusted deck they smiled at each other.

"He's still chasing lightning bugs," she said with so much affection in her voice, Matthew physically felt her smile.

"Well," he said, rising slowly to his feet.

She rose as well, hugging her arms around herself to ward off the late night chill that had settled in. Or was it to keep herself from reaching for him? he wondered.

In that moment he knew only one thing with certainty. He had to impose some space between them. A million miles ought to do it. "I guess I'd better take this little guy home and put him to bed. He's had a big day."

"I'd say we all have." Her gaze connected with his with an awareness and a longing neither could ignore any longer.

And somehow he just couldn't let it go at that. So many disclosures had been made that night. So many more had been left under wraps. So many feelings begged to be explored.

"Katie . . ."

The soft yearning in her eyes had him taking a step toward her. Hard-won resistance crowded in to replace the yearning and stopped him at the last second, a mere breath away. For her sake as well as his own he didn't finish what never should have been started. He didn't indulge in the sweet, pulsing desire to wrap her in his arms. Didn't satisfy the need to taste those full, parted lips and drown in the summer-fresh scent of her skin.

And he didn't die a little with wanting to do all those things and more. Like hell he didn't.

Summoning all his strength and a leaky shipload of arguments about why things couldn't be between them, he touched a hand to her hair, then tugged gently. "Thanks, Katie-did." Hearing the gruffness in his voice, he tried again, shooting for light and airy. "The burgers were great. The company was even better . . . even if you don't know your fifties from your sixties."

"I knew you weren't finished gloating," she said. But her smile was obviously forced, and her heart, like his, just wasn't in her teasing.

Careful not to wake Joey, Matthew picked him up, blanket and all, and cradled him against his chest. "I'll return the blanket in the morning."

"Whatever." She waved a hand that said don't worry about it. "Just put that boy to bed. I think you could do with some sleep too.

"We'll have to do this again sometime when Lisa can join us," she added, working over-hard at sounding casual and full of neighborly love.

"Right," he agreed in the same forced tone, and stepped off the deck, not daring to turn and face her. "We'll do that. 'Night, Katie."

"G'night," she called softly. "Oh, and Matthew?"

He stopped in his tracks and braced himself.

"Five bucks says it was 1959."

Shaking his head in disbelief, he chuckled and marched on home. Leave it to her, he thought, to use an argument to diffuse a tense moment instead of compound it. Somehow, he didn't think it was supposed to work that way. But then, nothing ever worked the way it was supposed to around Katie.

FOUR

Katie found out Sunday evening that Matthew had lied to her about one thing. He *did* do first aid. He just didn't like it. He especially didn't like doing it on her.

She hadn't been surprised when she'd stumbled across her backyard and into his to see charcoal smoke drifting lazily up from his grill. She hadn't even been surprised to see the woman she now knew was Lisa relaxed on a deck chair, looking regal and composed and like she belonged there.

What *had* surprised her was the look of utter horror that whitened Matthew's face to a sickly shade of tapioca when he caught sight of her.

"What the—"

"Oh, gosh . . ." Eyes wide and apologetic, Katie stopped, her gaze darting disjointedly between Matthew and Lisa. "I—I'm sorry. I—I didn't mean to interrupt anything," she stammered as she clutched the tea towel higher around her hand in an attempt to staunch the blood flow. With a supreme effort, she pasted on her best it's-really-nothing smile and started backing toward her yard. "If you'll just dial 911, I'll go back and wait for . . . for . . ."

"For God's sake, Katie!" Matthew shouted, shaking out of his shock. He tossed the spatula and sprinted toward her. "What . . . Oh, Lord." When he got a good look at the blood soaking the towel and running down her arm, he scooped her into his arms.

"Matthew. This really isn't . . . necessary. It's just a little . . . cut."

"Right. Nothing a major transfusion can't set right," he said caustically. "You little fool. What have you done to yourself now? You're bleeding to death. And for what? What needed fixing this time, Katie, that couldn't have waited? Don't answer that, I don't want to know. Look at her!" he demanded of Lisa as he marched up the deck steps.

Lisa was doing a lot of looking, Katie noticed, as Matthew, swearing under his breath, shouldered his way through the sliding doors and into his kitchen.

Katie had to admit she did feel a little dizzy. From loss of blood, maybe. From a touch of shock, probably. From Matthew's intense proximity, definitely. Despite the fact that he was yelling at her and doing some trembling of his own, his arms felt warm and secure wrapped around her.

"Matthew, really," she began, trying to put him at ease. "It's not—"

"Shut up. Just shut up. Dammit, Katie! I *knew* you were going to do something like this to yourself someday." His words were hard and scolding. His eyes and hands, however, were gentle and caring as he sat her in a kitchen chair and eased her arm onto the table top.

Peripherally aware of Lisa joining them, Katie cast her a regretful look. "I'm really sorry to barge in like this. It's just . . . I couldn't seem to get it to stop bleeding."

Matthew peeled back the towel and exploded. "An artery. She hit an artery!"

"What can I do?"

Lisa's voice, concerned yet in complete control, lent a sense of calm. Matthew wasn't in a borrowing mood, though. With quick, brusque motions and even more brusque words, he showed Lisa where to apply pressure while he fashioned a makeshift tourniquet, cursing Katie and her antics all the while.

Over the top of Matthew's head, Katie saw Lisa's sympathetic smile. Her intent to hate Lisa on sight died a swift, painless death. She smiled back, recognizing the kindness in the other woman's eyes as sincere.

"Didn't I tell you, Lisa?" Matthew grumbled nonstop as he worked efficiently yet furiously over her hand. "Didn't I tell you she'd do herself in someday with her bull-headed, harebrained antics?"

Some of the color had returned to his face, Katie noted. None of the concern, however, had left. He really was overreacting. Kind of like the way Danny, her sister Maggie's husband, reacted each time Maggie went into labor. As though if anything happen to her, he'd throttle her. He loved Maggie very much, Danny did.

On that flash of insight, Katie's heart pumped a few more quarts through the old bloodstream. She eyed Matthew skeptically and decided from the dark scowl on his face that blood loss must be affecting her reasoning powers. That was *not* the look of love. Which, of course, she didn't want it to be. Not even a little.

"Let me guess," he said, blasting through her thoughts, which she suspected were shock driven. "You were sharpening the blades on your chain saw so you could do a little recreational pruning. Or was it, let's see, I bet you were cleaning your ceiling fans and thought you could do a better job of it if you left them running on high speed."

"Matthew, I—"

"Better yet, you've just been itching to overhaul that lawn mower—"

"Matthew!"

"What?" he barked, all his worry and panic and frustration erupting in that single word.

"I was washing dishes!" she shouted back.

"See?" he said to Lisa, who had been listening to

the exchange, smiling a measuring little smile. "Did I tell you she was nuts? I *knew* it would be something stupid. Can you believe it? She was actually—" he paused mid-tirade and whipped his head back to Katie. The furrow between his brows deepened. "Washing dishes?" he finished limply.

She nodded. "Broke a glass."

He drew a deep breath, then let it out slowly. "Oh."

"Yeah, oh," she repeated, as their eyes spoke to each other of embarrassment, understanding, forgiveness, and even, in the aftermath, reluctant humor.

He was the first to smile. She was the first to notice the room had grown very quiet and that Lisa was watching them with dedicated interest.

"Well," Matthew said, finally tuning in to the tension around them. "I think we've stopped the bleeding. How does it feel?"

Aware of Lisa's scrutiny and of a gentling in Matthew she was sure he was *not* aware of, Katie pasted on a brave smile. "Fine. It feels fine. Really, really fine. It really is a little cut. Just poorly placed. Really bad luck, huh?" She sounded like the original Rambling Rose. A really, really rambling Rambling Rose. She knew it, but she couldn't stop it.

"I'll just go slap a Band-Aid on it and it'll be as good as new. Thanks, you two. Cute couple. Really cute. You just go on back to your steaks—they sure smell good, by the way—and I'll get out of your hair. Gee,

I'm sorry I missed telling Joey good-bye. You tell him that when you talk to him, okay? Well." She paused and smiled brightly. "Here I go."

Good to her word, she stood up—and she was gone. Really, really gone.

Katie woke up to sterile white walls and blinding lights. After the moment it took for her to reconstruct the events of her day, she realized she must be in a hospital emergency room. The only logical conclusion as to why she was in the hospital was that she'd passed out colder than a cod in a supermarket freezer. Oh, boy.

She turned her head on the pillow and saw Matthew. Her eyes moistened at the weary, worried look of him. Sitting beside her gurney, elbows propped on wide-spread thighs, head dropped into his hands, his fingers were plowing recklessly through that wealth of summer-wheat-colored hair as he stared at the floor.

Her heart went all soft and mush. "Hey, you," she whispered.

His head jerked up. The look in his eyes spoke of pure panic . . . then sweet relief. He stood and touched a hand to her forehead as he made a determined attempt to smile. The hand, she noticed, was shaking. His voice wasn't much steadier.

"Hey yourself," he said in a ragged whisper. "Didn't

anyone ever tell you it's not polite to pass out in a man's kitchen and bleed all over his linoleum? That kind of behavior is not going to get you too many party invitations."

She was so sorry. Not just about the mess in his kitchen, but for the scare she'd given him. In his eyes she could see echoes of all the fear and pain he'd felt another time, for another woman. Of endless days and nights of waiting by the side of a hospital bed, until one day the waiting gave way to death and a new kind of pain was born.

Tears again came unbidden. Tears that he mistook as those of her own physical pain.

"Oh, baby, are you hurting? I'll get someone in here right away."

She clutched his arm when he headed for the curtain that passed for a door. "No. No. I'm fine. I just feel so . . . stupid. I can't believe I did that to you. I've never fainted in my life!"

His shoulders relaxed with her reassurances. Moving back beside her, he gave her one of his crooked, melting smiles, which made a major improvement in her lowered blood pressure.

"For a first time, you pulled it off with a remarkable degree of skill," he said. "That header you took onto the table was a beaut."

She groaned and rolled eyes. "Well, you know me. Anything worth doing is worth doing well."

His eyes softened. And so, if possible, did his voice. And his touch as he stroked his thumb across her cheek. "So. No smoke screens now, Katie. How are you? Really."

She thought about it for a moment, made sure all her moving parts were working, and flexed her neatly bandaged hand. "Fine. I really do feel fine."

"Think you can sit up without keeling over?"

"Think you've got one more catch in you if I can't?"

"Let's hope it doesn't come to that. But if it does, I won't let you fall."

So where were you when I was falling in love with you? she asked silently as their eyes met. He hadn't caught her then and set her right. And where had she been, she asked herself grimly, when they were handing out common sense?

She broke eye contact abruptly and introduced a much-needed perspective to the moment.

"Poor Lisa," she said as he helped her to a sitting position. "She must be furious because I spoiled your evening."

"Let's worry about Katie right now, okay? Lisa can take care of herself."

"She was very nice. Even prettier up close than from a distance." She watched his eyes for signs she didn't want to see, but his face was a mask of determined concern.

"Yeah. She's very nice and very pretty. Now will you concentrate on what you're doing?"

The curtain shimmied open and a white jacket and a clipboard breezed into the room. "Well, she's up," the owner of the jacket and clipboard pronounced cheerfully. "How's she doing?"

"*She* is doing just fine," Katie said in the same cheerful tone, working hard to tamp down her irritation. "And you can direct your questions to her as if she's a real, functioning person."

The good doctor didn't miss a beat. "Has a bit of an attitude, doesn't she?" He grinned and shoved a thermometer in her mouth before she could fire back a retort.

He took a quick pulse check, eyeballed her pupils, and patted her on the knee. "She can go home. I can give her something for the pain, but I'm afraid I can't do a thing for that attitude." He whipped the thermometer out of her mouth.

She was quick. "Smart a—"

Matthew was too. "Thanks, Doc," he said loudly, and shot a warning glare at Katie. "Any special instructions?"

"Take her home and put her to bed. She'll be nice as new tomorrow. Oh, and hide her crystal so she can't pull this stunt again." With that little tidbit of advice, he handed Matthew the prescription and breezed out as fast as he'd come in.

"Well," she grumbled as Matthew helped her off the gurney, "I hope his bill is as brief as his visit."

"Come on," he said, slipping an arm around her shoulders for support. "Let's get her home before he decides to look in on her again and bring his big needle with him."

Snuggling into the curve of his arm, she slipped an arm around his waist. "It's really not nice to pick on the walking wounded."

His reaction was as unguarded as hers as he tucked her in close and dropped a kiss on the top of her head. "It's your own fault for being so much fun to pick on."

Matthew's teasing was gentled by concern on the ride home. He became all business, though, when he tucked her into bed. Lisa had been watching for them and joined them when they pulled into the drive. Standing by Katie's bed beside Matthew, she held out a glass of water and a pain pill.

"All this fuss for an itsy-bitsy puncture wound," Katie groused as she reluctantly swallowed the medication. "In a couple of days, I'll never know there was anything wrong."

"In a couple of days," Matthew said sternly, "you can prove you're good as new. Today, tonight specifically, you're going to stay in that bed if I have to tie you in it."

"Fine. Fine. I'll stay put. Just go and finish your dinner. I really am sorry, Lisa," she added, glancing past Matthew at the other woman. "You've been awfully generous about this."

Lisa smiled kindly. "Don't worry about it. I'm just glad it wasn't serious."

Matthew stared down at her, obviously reluctant to leave. "Is there anything else I can get you before we go?"

She shook her head. "No. Just go. And quit worrying about me. I'm fine."

"How about I come back over in an hour or so and check in on you?"

"Not necessary. I'll probably be out like a light."

Still he lingered.

"Matthew, I'm fine. And I can take care of myself. Tell him, Lisa. Us girls are made of tough stuff."

He rolled his eyes. Katie sensed that only with great difficulty did he swallow his opinion about the accuracy of that statement as it pertained to her.

"Call if you need," he said instead.

"I won't need. Now go."

With a final, concerned scowl, he did.

Lisa smiled again and gave Katie a conspiratorial wink as she followed him out the door.

Katie returned her smile. In fact, she was still sitting there with that bright false smile on her face when the first tear slipped down her cheek.

It had taken until that moment to set in. Matthew and Lisa were perfect together.

And she was better off on her own.

Sometimes, though, she wished it wasn't so lonely, this business of being alone.

"I managed to salvage the steaks," Lisa was saying as Matthew walked straight through the house to the kitchen and snagged a beer from the refrigerator. He was strictly a social drinker these days and hadn't felt the need for a good stiff shot of anything in a couple of years. Tonight, though, a double hit of Scotch would have done nicely.

He settled for the beer, twisted off the top, and pulled a long, deep swallow before turning to Lisa. For the first time since he'd caught sight of Katie, bleeding and shocky as she stumbled into his yard, he thought about how the events had affected Lisa. She'd been a brick.

"I'm sorry about all this," he said, shrugging help-lessly.

"Apologies are just running rampant around here, aren't they?" She smiled. "Actually, it wasn't a total loss. Rather enlightening, if you want to know the truth. After hearing you talk all evening about Katie and her exploits, I was eager to meet her."

He frowned when he realized she was right. He *had* been talking about Katie all night.

Lisa's eyebrows raised in an amused reaction to his scowl. "Matthew, she's adorable."

He took another long swallow, hoping to stanch the flood of emotions that had been flowing like Katie's blood. She'd looked so hurt, so helpless. He shook off the memory and flashed Lisa a tight smile. "Yeah, she's a real cute kid."

Lisa had very kind, very wise eyes. They saw too much sometimes. Now was one of those times. "She's hardly a kid."

He shrugged as if to say he hadn't really thought about it. "Yeah, well, she acts like one sometimes."

"A quirk you find refreshing?" she asked, eyeing him thoughtfully.

He considered that. "A quirk I find exasperating."

"Hmm," was all she said as she set their dinner on the table.

She left shortly after they ate, on the pretext of having an early morning production meeting at the TV studio where she worked as an associate producer of the noon news show. Matthew suspected her meeting wasn't that early. Lisa never could lie worth a damn. She was leaving because he was lousy company.

He felt guilty that he'd been so distracted, but there hadn't been a thing he could do about it. Lisa had understood and was giving him the room he needed. In fact, her last words were in reference to his distraction.

"I think you'd feel better if you checked in on her

before you turn in. Wouldn't want all that first aid to go for naught." Then she kissed him on the cheek and hugged him good-bye.

He stood in the doorway and watched her go, feeling like a fraud. He'd thought of nothing but Katie since he'd left her. Lisa hadn't been fooled for a minute. What must she be thinking? And what, he wondered, was he going to do about Katie?

He dragged a hand through his hair, shut and locked the door, then headed for the kitchen. There was nothing to do there. It was, thanks to Lisa, as neat and tidy as the proverbial pin. Just like his life would be if he married her.

Hating himself for the trace of dismay that notion triggered, he walked out onto the deck. Bracing his palms on the railing, he listened to the night sounds and told himself he wasn't going to check on his neighbor.

A few minutes later he let himself in her back door.

"You're supposed to be asleep."

Katie looked up from the book she was reading and broke into a wide, welcoming smile. Her blond hair fell recklessly about her face, her cheeks and eyes burned beacon-bright, and as usual, her T-shirt was far too tight.

"Hiiieee!" she said cheerfully. Very cheerfully. In fact, he'd never known anyone so glad to see him.

Patting the bed covers beside her hip, she scooted over and made room for him to sit down. "What are you doing here?"

"I'm checking on you," he said, ignoring her invitation and the gut-knotting bouncing that was going on beneath that damn T-shirt as she scooted around on the bed. He planted his feet more firmly on the threshold. "I told you I'd be back."

"I'll be back," she mimicked in her best Terminator voice, then giggled like a kid. "Hey, I did that pretty good, didn't I? Or was it well? I did that pretty well." She tried it again. "I'll be back." She grinned, then looked up at him as if she'd forgotten he was there. The words that came out of her mouth and the surprise in her eyes confirmed that she had. "Matthew. Hiiieee! What are you doing here?"

Here we go again. Matthew frowned, wondering what the devil was wrong with her. A glance at the prescription bottle on her nightstand provided his answer.

"Katie, honey, did you buy any chance take another pain pill?"

"Pain pill? Pain pill?" she repeated, sounding like a perplexed parrot. Her gaze followed his, albeit dazedly, to the bottle. "Oh. Oh, you mean these? These—let's see, what are they?" She eyed the bottle, then squinted as she tried to pronounce the name of the medication. "Perc . . . Perc . . . Perca-doodledoooo!" she crowed in delight, then doubled over, collapsing on her side in a fit of hysterical laughter.

"Percodan," Matthew said as he grabbed the bottle and capped it. "Pretty strong stuff for a lightweight. Can one assume," he went on, giving in and easing a hip onto the bed, "that you're not used to taking medication?"

She popped up to a sitting position, her expression puzzled but pensive. "I took an aspirin once. Made me dizzy."

He sighed deeply and hung his head. "Katie, Katie, what am I going to do about you?"

"I don't know," she said, matching his solemn tone. "But Chase would know what to do."

His head snapped up. "Chase?" he repeated, feeling a swift and unacceptable flash of jealousy at the mention of another man's name.

Her smile was both consoling and serene as she patted his hand in reassurance, then reached for the book she'd set aside when he'd come in. He could see from the cover it was one of those romance novels that were so popular these days.

So she wanted him to think she didn't believe in romance, he mused. Why then, he wondered with a sharp tug in the vicinity of his heart, was she reading about someone else's?

He watched in thoughtful silence as with serious—if a bit dismantled—intensity, she thumbed through the book until she found what she was looking for. Then she began reading aloud and with great dramatic flare:

"Chase's eyes shot a dark, sensual heat across the room when he spotted Carmella. The pale alabaster of her bare shoulders was backlit by candlelight, bathed in the fire's glow. One look and he knew exactly what he had to do. He had to have her. Right then. Right there. Trembling with his desire for her, he—"

Matthew snatched the book from her hands and snapped it shut. "I get the picture," he said, and did a little trembling of his own.

"Well," she said, all guileless suggestion and drugged innuendo. "Then you know what to do."

He knew all right. He knew he had to get out of there before the temptation to accept the invitation she so openly extended won out over common decency. Before he forgot she wasn't in his plans and that any kind of physical intimacy with her would be wrong. Before he took complete and total advantage of her near comatose state.

"Katie," he said gently, then reached for her when he realized she was listing heavily to starboard.

He grasped her shoulders, intending to lay her back down and tuck her safely under her covers. But they were so fragile, those shoulders, so fine-boned and delicate . . . and so at odds with the strength of the spirited woman who was launching herself into his arms like a guided missile.

She was stronger than she looked. Faster too. And she had the advantage of surprise on her side. He was flat on his back, held in a death grip, before he had a chance to holler "Timber!" Not that he wanted to. He liked where he landed just fine.

Her slim body was spread like liquid silver over the length of his. The gentle weight of her breasts was pressed flat against his chest, and that riot of tumbling blond curls spilled across his face like fine French silk.

She lifted her head and met his eyes with willful and wanton—if a bit woozy—wonder. "Do you want to kiss me, Matthew?" she whispered breathlessly.

He swallowed and tried to shake his head no. A tough trick when his mouth had already formed the word yes.

She looked momentarily perplexed. "Do you want *me* to kiss *you*?"

He couldn't swallow past the groan in his throat as her gaze strayed from his eyes to his mouth. She wet her lips, sucked the lower one beneath her teeth, then smiled a slow, wondrous smile when she felt his involuntary affirmation against her belly. "I think you do," she said, her eyes sparkling with an intoxicating mixture of happiness and awe. "I think I will."

Who was he to say no to a lady? After all, she was only talking about a kiss. He could handle it. And with a little luck, she'd never remember what a heel he'd been for taking advantage of her.

But it was incredibly potent, that kiss, and heartbreakingly romantic. Just twenty-four hours earlier, in the soft suspense of a warm spring night, she'd claimed she didn't believe in romance. He'd silently agreed.

That was then. This was now . . . and right now, she was making a believer of both of them.

Sweetly parted, softly yearning, her lips met his with a hint of surprise, a whisper of temptation, and the heat of a hundred summer nights. Romance was definitely on her mind.

Somewhere between her vulnerability and what he was beginning to recognize as his own, he got lost in the taste of her mouth and the wild and restless awakening of her body. The kiss deepened and lengthened, and he simply couldn't stop it. He wove his fingers through her hair and sought more intimacy.

When he wooed her tongue with his, she answered. When he promised with his throaty moans, she trembled and nothing in the world could have made him push her away.

On a breathy sigh, she took care of the problem for him. She pulled back and smiled. It was a devastatingly angelic smile. But a provocative siren's smile too. "See," she said, sounding breathless and victorious. "You *do* know what to do."

"Lord, Katie," he whispered as his body reacted

with a vengeance. Oh, yes, he knew exactly what he wanted to do with her.

Trouble was, she knew exactly what she wanted to do with him too. She wanted to drive him crazy. And she was doing a damn fine job of it.

One minute she was seducing him like an Amazon priestess with a mating ritual on her mind, and the next, the very next, she was pressing her face into his shoulder and crying as if her heart were broken.

He stiffened, confused, before passion took a back-seat to concern. "Katie, sweetheart, what is it? Does your hand hurt? Did I hurt you?" He shifted carefully so she was on her back and he was braced on an elbow above her. Brushing the hair from her eyes, he urged her to tell him what was wrong.

"I'm so s-sorry," she wailed between sobs. "So sorry."

"Sorry? You have nothing to be sorry for, sweetheart. You're the one who's hurt."

"No. It—it hurt you too. I s-saw the look in your eyes. In the hospital. You were re-remembering. Your wife. Your pain. I'm s-sorry I made you hurt again. I'd never w-want to make you hurt. Never."

Stunned, shaken, Matthew pulled her into his arms and held her. Moved by her emotions and denying the intensity of his own, he buried his face in her hair and murmured words of comfort. And he fought the notion that she was right. That he was the one in need. That waiting there by her side in that hospital that smelled of antiseptic and of life and of death hadn't dredged up memories too painful to deal with, feelings too powerful to forget.

In the end, whether it was her need or his own that he was tending, it didn't matter. What mattered, he realized as he held her, was that for this moment, this particular place in time, this was where he wanted to be.

Later, much later, when her sighs had grown heavy and her heartbeat slowed with sleep, he lay down beside her. He didn't even think about leaving her alone. He simply wrapped her in his arms and held her and stroked her . . . and thought of Carol.

There, in the darkness of Katie McDonald's bedroom, in the light of her gentle spirit, he listened to the silence of the night and the memories of his past.

He, too, did some crying . . . and some goodbyeing . . . and finally, allowing his feelings for this woman to guide him, he did some letting go.

FIVE

The dinner had gone quite well, Katie thought in retrospect as she dried the last plate and put it away. The roast had turned out perfectly, the glazed carrots were deliciously rich, and the chocolate mousse had been a real hit with Joey. And she'd accomplished exactly what she'd set out to do. She'd invited the three of them, Matthew, Joey, and Lisa, to her home as if they were already a family unit.

It had been exactly the right thing to do. The gesture had sanctioned the arrangement for everyone to see, cemented the future into fact with her acknowledgment.

Lisa really was very nice, Katie mused. She and Matthew looked terrific together. And Joey liked Lisa, too, she could tell. That was good. They were going to make a wonderful family, she told herself bracingly.

So why did she feel lower than a pothole in a gravel road?

Because it had darn near killed her to see Lisa and Matthew sitting side by side at her table. Lisa's subtle elegance played beautifully off Matthew's diamond-in-the-rough casualness. They looked comfortable together. Perfectly suited. Lisa was everything he needed in a wife and everything Joey needed in a mother. In short, they had family-ever-after written all over them.

Katie had never felt more on the outside looking in. She just wished it hadn't hurt so much to see them as a family. She wished that every time she had glanced at Matthew she hadn't had to remind herself that he was something she couldn't have. Look but don't touch. Long for but don't expect. Love but don't show it.

"McDonald," she muttered aloud when she realized she'd wrung the dishtowel into a knot of soggy cotton. "Shape up already. This poor-me stuff is playing a little thin. And admit it. Love has nothing to do with it. It's more a question of chemistry. And maybe a little loneliness."

Besides, hadn't Matthew made his feelings perfectly clear? Since the day two weeks earlier when she'd cut her hand, he had imposed a distance between them that hadn't been there before. Oh, he'd checked in on her the next morning before he'd left for work, if you could call "Hi, you're looking better," checking in. He had looked exceptionally tired himself, as if he hadn't slept much that night. Before she'd had a chance to comment on it, he'd breezed on out the door.

Maybe it had been his way of letting her know he didn't appreciate her constant intrusions into his life. She couldn't blame him. She really hadn't planned for all those things to happen and to involve him. They had just happened.

Since that morning and their brief conversation when she'd called to invite the three of them to dinner, she'd only seen him in passing—if you didn't count the night she'd accidentally sprayed him when she was washing her car.

That particular memory made her grin. Lord, he'd wanted to be mad. He'd wanted to get even. She'd been looking forward to his method when he'd promptly turned on his heel, mumbled something under his breath, then hightailed it into his house.

As she'd stood there watching him go, the limp hose dangling from her hand, she'd realized she'd been foolish even to fantasize about loving Matthew Spencer. And "fantasize" was the only word for it. Love, or even a reasonable facsimile thereof, was never supposed to be a factor in her life anyway. That's why that night's dinner had been so important. It had given her necessary perspective.

Tossing the dishtowel on the counter, she headed for her bedroom, angry that she had to remind herself continually that Matthew was off-limits. She'd known that from the outset. Not just because of Lisa, although she would never boogie on another woman's dance floor, but because she'd realized from the first moment she'd seen him that he was way too much man for her. He was too handsome, too intense, too much fun, too much everything.

And she was too little. She was not wife and mother material. She'd proven that once already. The mother part, at any rate. It only followed that the wife part wouldn't be a strength either.

Stripping off her clothes, she headed for the bathroom and a long hot soak while she added more evidence to the case she was building against herself.

"I mean, really, McDonald," she said aloud as she dumped bath salts into the tub. "Couldn't you just see yourself being introduced to the Handcocks of Prospect Boulevard?" Why, they'd take one look at her rebel-with-a-thousand-causes expression, read up on the little pickles she sometimes got herself into, and tell Matthew to trade her in for a fish worth keeping. A nice, respectable, well-bred, politically correct fish who would make the perfect splash in the society pond and a perfect mother for Joey.

The perfect mother. The pain that always accompanied that phrase sliced deeper than she usually let it. For a tight, aching moment, she made herself feel the hurt. She needed the reminder that she'd had her chance to prove what kind of a mother she would be. In every aspect, she'd failed.

Toweling dry, she told herself she was glad she'd forced the encounter so she could see Lisa and Matthew and Joey together. Besides, the dinner had been the very least she could do to make amends for the disastrous way she'd intruded on Matthew and Lisa's evening together two weeks ago.

Her hand was fine now. With the exception of a little muddling of her memory during and after her quick trip to the emergency room, all was back to normal.

Except that she hurt. Bone-deep, heart-sore, soul-wrenching hurt.

It was too early to go to bed, but she was too weary to dwell on Matthew anymore. She crawled between the sheets and switched on the radio. The mournful lyrics of "One Is the Loneliest Number" swelled into the room, matching her mood. The single tear damp-ening her pillow proved just how much.

In the house next door Matthew was slumped mood-ily in a chair when Lisa walked out of Joey's bedroom. He raised a questioning eyebrow when she sat down in the chair next to his.

"He's fine," she assured him. "Just a bad dream. He's already asleep again."

Closing his eyes, he let his head fall back against the cushion in weary defeat.

"Don't be so hard on yourself, Matt. Sometimes it just takes a woman's touch to settle a little one down. It's this gift we have," she added. "Our chests are a lot softer to cuddle against than yours."

He gave her the smile he knew she wanted. "I hate seeing him like that. I hate not knowing what to do."

"I've got a feeling you'll be learning to handle bad dreams and a lot more before long."

"Yeah," he said, brightening marginally. "I guess I will at that. And you say it'll all fall into place?"

"A little practice, a little experience, and it'll be as second nature to you as building a house."

He met her eyes and this time his smile was genuine. "Well, wise lady, time, as they say, will tell. Meanwhile, can I get you something to drink?"

She stayed him with a hand on his knee when he started to rise. "No drink, Matthew. We need to talk."

Settling back into the chair, he watched her and waited, absently stroking his upper lip. Even before she began, he knew what she wanted to talk about. Katie. He just wasn't sure he was ready to hear it . . . or what he was going to say.

"You don't have to look like a fifth grader pulling detention," she said. "I'm not going to scold you."

Pushing out of the chair, he walked over to the

sliding doors leading to the deck, tucking his hands into the hip pockets of his pants.

For two long weeks he'd tried to stay away from Ms. Wreak-havoc-with-his-hormones McDonald. Tried to convince himself that she was nothing more than an intrusion on his time and energy . . . and his sleep. It hadn't worked. Going to her house for dinner was supposed to have shown both Katie and himself what a perfect little family he, Lisa, and Joey made. He should have known it would explode in his face like so many splitting atoms.

He looked toward Katie's yard, then back to Lisa, knowing he had to say something. "Lisa . . ."

When he stopped, she did what she always did best. She made it easy for him. "You've got it bad for her, haven't you?" she asked. Her voice held not a hint of anger, but a bounty of sympathetic humor.

The guilt and regret he felt must have been stamped on his face like a notary seal, for she smiled at him.

"It's all right, Matt. In fact, it's more than all right," she continued when he just stared at her. "It's special, this feeling that I sense you have for her. And Matt, it really is okay."

He scrubbed a hand over his jaw. "I don't know what to say. Hell, I don't even know what to do. I'd thought that you and I . . ." He trailed off again, still at a loss for words.

"I know what you thought. And I thought I wanted

it too. We both had something special once. You and Carol, Zack and I. We both know what it's like when that perfect match comes along and makes us complete. But we were wrong to think we should settle for the friendship we have to compensate for our losses. If Katie hadn't come along and opened your eyes, we might have made a terrible mistake. I'll always feel I owe her for that."

He was quiet for a long time before facing her again.

"There isn't any room for guilt here, Matt. The simple truth is that we were selling ourselves short by thinking what we had was enough. Seeing you with Katie makes me realize that. The way you light up when she looks at you has given me new hope of finding that kind of love again myself."

He smiled helplessly and gave up the fight. "That light you see is heartburn. The woman does things to my mind that set my stomach on fire."

"I'd say there are a few other things she sets ablaze, too, big guy." She laughed when he rolled his eyes. "Come over here and give me a hug and tell me she makes you happy."

"She makes me crazy," he growled, pulling Lisa into his arms and holding on tight. "What the hell am I going to do about her? And what am I going to do about the Handcocks?"

She pulled back, frowning at him. "Give Eunice

and Grant a little credit. Give Katie some credit too. If she can soften that hard heart of yours, she can soften a couple more."

"Hard-hearted? Me?" he asked, genuinely wounded.

She cupped his cheek in her palm. "Poor choice of words. Brokenhearted is more accurate. If she can mend your heart, she can work miracles."

"She's going to have to. I'll never risk losing my chance at getting Joey back, but I'm afraid I can't let Katie go either."

"You'll work it out. Together."

"You're a hell of a woman, Lisa Harding. I'm a fool to let you go."

"You'd be a bigger one if you didn't. And so would I if I stayed."

"You know I love you," he said, a world of regret coloring his words.

"I love you too. But I'm not *in* love with you and you're not in love with me, and lukewarm just isn't going to cut it anymore."

"How," he asked, amazed at the depth of her insight, "did you manage to make something I've been fighting since the day I laid eyes on Katie become so simple?"

"Because the right thing is always simple. And what you feel for Katie is right. Now work on it. I've got to go."

He ran a hand down her arm and linked his fingers with hers. "Dinner next week sometime?"

She squeezed his hand. "You're on. And I'll expect a progress report then. Something tells me that convincing Katie she's right for you is not going to be easy. She really is a charmer, Matt, but she seems dedicated to keeping her distance for your sake."

He grinned, already relishing the resistance he knew she'd put up.

"From the look on your face," Lisa said, "I'd say she doesn't have a prayer."

"Not an amen," he agreed. Slinging an arm around her shoulders, he walked Lisa to her car.

It was Matthew, however, who was doing the praying the next morning when he sidled over to Katie's on the pretext of bumming a cup of coffee.

Joey was sleeping late, and now that Matthew had made a commitment to see this through with Katie, he wanted to get on with it. Lisa was right. Things could work between them.

Katie had brought back everything he'd been missing in his life—excitement, emotion, good old-fashioned fun. He smiled to himself. Good old-fashioned lust. And love. Most of all love. The kind he'd never thought to have again when he'd lost Carol. And Katie would be good for Joey. Somehow he'd make the Handcocks see just how good. Somehow he'd make Katie see it too.

He figured he had an edge. The element of surprise was on his side. And he was on to her now. That little dinner party she'd orchestrated the night before had been an attempt to solidify the notion that she was strictly "buddy" material. The friendly fifth wheel.

She might have convinced him, too, if he hadn't seen the longing in her eyes every time she'd let herself glance his way. She loved him. He was sure of it. In fact, he'd known it from the beginning. All he had to do now was convince her it was okay.

Piece of cake, right, Spencer? Right. Eliminating the national debt would be the only challenge to even come close.

He was determined, though, and early morning seemed as good a time as any to catch her off guard. Only it wasn't a good time. Not for his libido, at any rate.

Katie was definitely up. Unfortunately, one look at her through the screen door off her deck and he was up too. Literally.

In bare feet, short shorts, and a tank top, with her hair in pigtails fastened high above each ear, she looked all of sixteen and as tempting as original sin. He should have outgrown this particular kind of reaction in his teens, he thought as he made a quick, painful adjustment to the fly of his jeans.

The radio was blaring, and she was baking and a-bopping and a-baying like a hound at a full moon.

Thank heavens she didn't have to make a living as a singer. She had a few moves, however, that if performed in public were certain to earn her some lucrative propositions.

Busy shucking and jiving and maneuvering a cookie sheet into the oven, she wasn't aware that he was standing outside her kitchen door watching her. Gentleman that he was, he took full advantage.

The Beatles, at full volume, were "shakin' it up," and Katie, at full throttle, was doing some shaking of her own. She bumped the oven door closed with her hip, then bounced across the room to the lively rock and roll beat.

She was having fun. He was having a stroke— maybe two—when she landed in the center of the room, facing him with her eyes closed, oven-mitt-clad hands waving above her head, hips swaying. She executed a shoulder shimmy that did amazing things for the front of her tank top and increased the pressure beneath his fly from moderate to acute. Tomorrow, he was going to buy her a bra. If he lived so long.

Out of sheer self-defense, he made a great production of clearing his throat.

Her eyes snapped open. She froze mid-gyration.

When an aching vulnerability replaced the surprise on her face, it took everything in him to stall the urge to haul her into his arms and love her insecurity away.

Since he knew she would never admit to any of those

feelings, he stayed put and let her take the lead . . . at least until she had him where he wanted to be.

Katie was a firm believer in age-old adages like "Life goes on," "Time heals all wounds," "Bake something, you'll feel better," and in her personal favorite, sixties music was the best cure for the blues.

She had been religiously practicing all of the above in an attempt to get over the previous night's doldrums, when she realized she had an audience.

Never more conscious of her bare feet, long legs, and off-key warbling, she promptly dropped her hands to her sides.

"So," she said to Matthew, shooting for snappy when she saw the amusement in his eyes, "you've got nothing better to do?"

"I don't believe I have," he drawled lazily.

The smile he gave her was nothing short of wicked. And devious. She swore she saw devious. It was either the devil in her or the one in his eyes that prompted her to challenge him.

"Well, hotshot, you know all the old songs, but do you know the moves too?"

His smile broadened into a cocky, I-don't-back-away-from-no-dare grin. "I think I remember a few. And I don't see any reason why you should be having all the fun."

She wasn't sure what she'd expected, but it wasn't for him to slide open the door, ease inside, and prove not only that he remembered the moves, but that he had a few new twists as well.

Before long she was dancing with him. And admiring. And forgetting, for a moment, that she wasn't supposed to be crazy about him.

"Hey, Ace, way to go! Patrick Swayze's got nothing on you." Right down to the dark T-shirt, snug, low-riding jeans, and tight, muscled buns, she added silently.

Laughing together, they bumped and grooved and twisted their way around her kitchen table, showing off their moves like teenagers at a sock hop.

They were both winded when the song wound down.

"I'll go one more round if you promise not to sing," he teased, a smile tugging at the corners of his mouth.

Not about to be bested, she met his challenge gamely. "My silence and your slur will cost you a buck. Shell out and you've got a deal."

But when the next song proved to be a slow ballad with too much romance and emotion that hit too close to the mark, she decided to beg off. She wasn't sure what was on his mind, but the look in his eyes made her a tiny bit nervous.

"Never learned to slow dance," she lied, backing away.

He saw through the lie and wasn't having any of it. Locking his gaze with hers, he pried his wallet out of his hip pocket, peeled out a dollar bill, and slapped it on the table. "Then it's past time you learned."

Feeling threatened by all that masculine appeal, all that sensual heat he seemed to be directing point-blank at her, she hedged. "The cookies—"

"Are fine," he interrupted, glancing at the timer, then back at her. "We've got five minutes, Katie. I can teach you a lot in five minutes."

She'd just bet he could—and would. Wearing a look that clearly warned, *Resist me and see where it gets you*, he latched on to her wrist. Stripping off her oven mitts and tossing them over his shoulder, he dragged her flush against him.

"The thing about slow dancing," he said in a velvety whisper that feathered across her face and sent about a zillion tingling explosions skittering along her skin, "is that you can make it anything you want it to be. A dance . . . " He moved slowly, sensuously, against her. "An adventure . . ." His hands, broad, strong, and warm, glided in a smooth, steady motion down the length of her back. There they claimed her hips and began kneading softly. "A seduction . . ."

"I—" She stopped and swallowed hard when he touched a particularly sensitive spot. "I opt for door number one."

He must have heard the panic in her voice, because

she felt his smile form against her cheek. "Sorry, Katie." He didn't sound sorry at all. "I'm afraid it's not your choice. You see, in a slow dance, the man leads. *I* get to call the shots. And I choose all three."

Awareness, as provocative as his whisper, as explosive as forbidden desire, hummed through her body like steamed heat. Reason, cause, and purpose must have slipped out the back door when she wasn't looking, because she didn't resist as he settled her closer still. Even her old standby, denial, was tempered by the discovery of all these feelings he was stirring to life. Left to fend for itself, it didn't stand much of a chance. Unless she did something. Fast.

"M-Matthew?"

"Hmmm?" he answered from somewhere in the vicinity of her earlobe. His hips and his hands, all of which were very busy south of her waist, were creating wonderful sensations that made her want to chuck resistance and get right down to defeat.

"Matthew . . . I, ah, I don't think . . . I mean . . . We need to talk about—about . . . What about Lisa?"

He pulled back and looked straight at her. The lazy heat she saw in his eyes took her breath away. The honest truth gave her reluctant hope.

"Lisa is a beautiful, wonderful woman. Don't look away from me, Katie," he demanded when she lowered her head. "She's my friend and I love her. But she's not the woman I love. And she's not the woman I want to make love to. Now, I hope we're through talking, because what I have in mind is a perfect end to this conversation."

Her panic was now pure and persistent as his words buzzed around inside her head like a swarm of mosquitoes scoping out the most vulnerable target. *Not the woman I love. Not the woman I want to make love to.*

Well, neither was she. He couldn't possibly mean her! No, no, no, no! Shaking her head, she tried to pull away. He held her fast and taught her a little more about the power of his persuasion.

Pressing his forehead to hers, he murmured her name. "It's time to give up the fight," he went on. "We tried it the other way. Friends, buddies. It didn't wash. I even tried to stay away from you. That didn't work either. The time for playing those particular games is over. It's time to move on to new ones. Ones with higher stakes."

She groaned miserably, feeling herself drift further and further toward the deep end of the pool. "Matthew . . . this just can't happen."

"It can," he insisted, and with the gentle pressure of his thumbs under her chin, tipped her face up to his and kissed the protest from her lips. At least he tried to.

"Matthew," she said again, the breathlessness of her voice telling her she was sinking fast. "This really *can't* happen."

"It's all right, Katie. It can and it will."

With soft, tantalizing nudges, he rimmed her lips with his tongue, seeking entry. Fire shot from the tips of her breasts to the pit of her belly as he sought and seduced and conquered.

"But I don't *want* this to happen," she whispered weakly, even as she snuggled close and wrapped her arms around his neck.

"I know, baby," he said while the smile she felt against her mouth told her he knew what a liar she was.

"Oh, Matthew . . ." She sucked in a harsh, needy breath as his wicked hands and hungry mouth combined in an assault that showed no mercy. "I—I want this to happen so badly, it hurts. What are we going to do?"

"I have a few thoughts on that topic."

She groaned as a thought or two of her own added more sparks to the fire. "You have *no* idea what you're letting yourself in for."

He answered her warning with another grin. When she buried her hands in his hair and opened her mouth for him again, he answered her invitation with a heart-pounding, muscle-melting, mind-mushing kiss.

The kiss went on and on, combining need and passion, denial and revelation, body and soul into a stunning collection of sensations that she couldn't have identified or named if her life depended on it. She knew only that she wanted it to go on forever. It would have, too, if Matthew hadn't had the good sense to come up for air. He broke the kiss just short of critical denial of oxygen.

"Katie?"

Eyes closed, head reeling, she sighed and dropped her forehead against his chest. "Ummmm?"

"I think your cookies might be burning."

"You can say that again." She felt his soft chuckle against her brow. Comprehension was slow to dawn. When it did, her eyes flew wide open and she snapped her head up. "Oh. Oh! My *cookie* cookies."

Bolting into action, she shoved him away. When her frantic search located a discarded oven mitt on the floor, she raced to the oven to rescue the cookies. A dozen charred lumps of something that resembled landscaping cinders stared back in accusatory silence.

"Damn!" she muttered, and slapped the sheet on the range top. "Look what you made me do. And where do you think you're going?" she snapped as she whirled around to see that perfect backside in those perfectly disreputable jeans make a slow retreat out her sliding door. "You think you can just waltz in here and . . . and . . ."

"And what?" he asked, grinning as he propped a hand on the door.

"Burn my cookies and get away with it?"

One bad-boy brow arched in victory. "I think I just did."

Hands on hips, she glared at him, trying to decide whether she wanted to kiss him again or force-feed him one of those lava rocks. The kiss won hands down.

He, however, wasn't going to give her the opportunity. "Just to show you how sorry I am—about the cookies, that is—I'm going to make it up to you." He checked his watch. "One o'clock sharp. Shorts'll do, and wear your high heeled sneakers, mama. The Spencer boys are going to take you to a party, Kansas City Royals style."

With that he trotted across her deck, leaving her to deal with her burnt cookies, her lit fuse, and a sense of dread that just wouldn't let go.

Like it or not, she was in love with him. He was in lust with her. And because of Joey, there was no common ground for them to meet in the middle.

The pile of peanut shells around Katie's feet had grown to end-loader proportions, Matthew noted with satisfaction. So had her enthusiasm—once she'd forgotten she was supposed to be guarding it. For a woman who had tried to convince him she didn't like baseball and wasn't about to horn in on their father-son outing, she was having the time of her life. So was he. So was Joey.

Congratulating himself on his powers of persuasion, Matthew paid the vendor for a second round of hot dogs to stave off Katie's delicate little appetite. He turned to hand one to her, then promptly ducked as she shot out of her seat, peanuts and popcorn flying. She shook her fist menacingly at the first-base umpire.

"Awweee geeezze . . . forthelubomike!" she said loudly around a mouthful of food. "Hewasafebyamile! Byamiile! Rrrruuublinndddd??? Iseblind???" she wailed, turning an infuriated and beleaguered glare at Matthew before she plopped back down in her seat with a disgusted thud.

Joey, watching her with an expression somewhere between awe and concern, turned wary eyes to his father. "Is she all right?"

At the end of the third inning, when he'd discovered her saucy little nose was taking on a pink tinge from the sun, Matthew had bought her a Royals baseball cap. Embarrassment painted her cheeks even pinker now. Matthew grinned as she tugged the cap's bill lower over her face in an attempt to disappear.

Much as he loved the look of her, he decided to help her out . . . a little. Pulling a studiously authoritative face, he eased into his father-son lecture mode and addressed Joey. "Remember yesterday when you were asking me what a poor sport was? Well, son, before we came today, I asked Katie to give us a demonstration of poor sportsmanship to clear that little matter for you.

"Nice job, McDonald," he added, his brisk nod

saying, "job well done." "Don't think you left a doubt in the boy's mind, right, Joey?"

"Is she going to boo and call the umpire bad names?" Joey asked.

Matthew leaned around his son to Katie, all innocence and interest. "That part of the demonstration, Katie?" She sank lower in her seat. "No? Well, I think you got your message across without it."

He felt a little guilty about teasing her. And a little sorry about quieting her down. But she was so much fun to tease. And so much fun to be with. He shouldn't have worried, though. Demure didn't suit Katie any more than dull did. By the seventh-inning stretch, she was back to her naturally animated self, singing—Lord help them all—"Take Me out to the Ball Game" along with the organ as she dove into another bag of peanuts.

"Don't you wanna come with us to meet my gramma and grampa, Katie?" Joey asked as they pulled into Matthew's drive around twilight.

Matthew watched her from behind the steering wheel as she looked down at the mustard and ketchup stains decorating her shirt. She ran a hand over the snarls springing from beneath her baseball cap and sent him a pleading look over Joey's head.

"Maybe next time, sport," Matthew said, sensing from her silence that she wasn't ready to take that big a step. "Katie's a little wiped out right now. I think maybe we wore her out."

"We didn't, did we Katie?"

"'Fraid so, kiddo," she said, giving the bill of Joey's cap an affectionate tug. "But I can't remember when I had so much fun. You're a real good time, you know that?"

"What about me?" Matthew asked. "Am I a good time too?"

She pasted on a perky grin. "The best. I'll take out a loan tomorrow to repay you for all the food you plied me with today."

He smiled. "Every man, woman, and child with a food concession is going to be on the lookout for you next game. A couple more hauls like today's and they'll be scoping out retirement property in Florida."

"Must have been the fresh air and sunshine," she said, looking a little sheepish as she slid out of the car.

Her false bravado didn't fool him for a minute. She was still running scared from what had happened in her kitchen that morning.

"It really was a fun afternoon, guys," she added, bending down to peer into the front seat. "'Bye, Joey. See you in a couple of weeks."

"'Bye, Katie. You look real neat in your cap."

Touching a hand to her head, she darted a self-conscious glance at Matthew.

"Yeah, Katie. You look real neat."

Her eyes softened before she dropped her lashes and hid them from his view. "The word 'neat' wouldn't stand within ten feet of me right now. See ya, guys," she said, backing away. "I've got a hot date with a washing machine and a bathtub."

"And don't forget about later," Matthew said.

Her gaze flashed warily back to his. "Later?"

"Later," he said meaningfully. "We started a . . . 'conversation' this morning, remember? I sort of had it in mind to finish it tonight."

He could see by the look on her face that she was thinking of finishing something, too, but not to the same end he had planned.

Run, Katie, run, he urged her silently. From involvement, commitment, love . . . whatever. After the way she'd come apart in his arms that morning, the way he'd come alive just holding her, she could run to Tibet if she wanted to. He'd dog her every step of the way.

SIX

The problem with men, Katie decided after her bath, as she slipped into clean shorts and a fresh T-shirt, was that they never did what they were supposed to do.

Take Matthew, for example, she continued as she plopped down in front of her vanity mirror. He was supposed to recognize trouble when he saw it and head in the opposite direction. He was supposed to marry Lisa and live happily ever after.

He *wasn't* supposed to boogaloo into her kitchen, kiss her until she short-circuited, then shanghai her into a family outing that left her wishing for things like—oh, Lord, it hurt even to think it—commitment, love, and everlasting.

"Okay," she grumbled aloud. "And sex. He makes me think about sex. Happy now?" she asked the gods of perpetual torment as she dragged a brush through her still-damp hair.

She couldn't get within ogling distance of Matthew and not think about what it would be like to make love to him. Couldn't recall his "dance steps" and the smooth glide of his hands on her body without wanting to "dance" with him again. Horizontally.

She glanced nervously at the clock on her bedside stand. Nine P.M. Matthew should be getting home from delivering Joey to his grandparents any minute now.

Joey. She dropped her head into her hands. She would do anything to keep from hurting that little boy. She'd grown to love him as much as she loved his father.

Her head shot up and she met her reflection in the mirror. "Did you say the L word again?"

Her face, its nose red from too much sun, its cheeks scarlet from too much discovery, its eyes heavy with guilt and defeat, confirmed it. Yes, she had.

"That's it, McDonald." Slapping both palms flat on the vanity, she squared off with the ninny in the mirror. "This was supposed to be settled. It ends here, do you understand? You *will* not, *can*not, and *do* not want this to go any further. When he waltzes back over here tonight and insists on resuming your 'conversation,' you're going to make that man see the light if you have to set him under a floodlight to do it."

She was ready for him when he rapped a knuckle on her sliding glass door ten minutes later. Every light in the house was on. The coffee was hot, and she'd tuned the radio to a polka station that was sure to stomp into dust any leftover notions he might have about finishing their slow dance.

Pasting on a perky, hands-off smile, she tugged open the door, took one look at his tortured expression, and flew into his arms.

So much for keeping her distance.

"Matthew, what is it?" she asked when he'd loosened his hold enough for her to breathe.

"Just let me hold you for a while."

Tucking her against his hip, he steered her into her living room and tugged her down with him onto the sofa, where he wrapped himself around her again.

After her initial shock at seeing the anguish darkening his face, she realized what had him so upset. She didn't need a degree in psychology to understand what was going on.

"It was tough, huh?" she asked.

Sighing deeply, he propped his chin on the top of her head. "Leaving him is always tough. And it just keeps on getting tougher."

Heartache bred heartache.

Hurting for him, and for her, she forced herself to pull away from his embrace. "You'll have him back with you soon," she said, determined to make him see reason. "You'll have him back, but you've got to stay the course."

He frowned down at her. "Stay the course?"

"The Handcocks? Lisa? Family of the year?"

He closed his eyes and shook his head. "Look, Katie, I know I came on fast and strong this morning . . ."

Here it comes, she thought, bracing herself. He was going to agree with her, tell her he was sorry. That he'd lost his head and lost his cool. That he didn't know what had gotten into him and leaving Joey that night had made him realize his mistake.

". . . and I know," he went on, "that I haven't given you a chance to get used to the idea, so let's get something straight right now."

Swallowing back her pain, she covered his hand with hers. "You don't have to explain. I know what your priorities are. I've known from the beginning. Joey is what is important here. And as far as this morning goes, hey, what's a little haywire hormones among friends?"

He stared at her. And just kept on staring while she sat there with a pathetic smile planted on her face and worked overhard at batting back the tears.

"Haywire hormones?" he repeated. "You think this is about hormones?"

"Well . . . sure. I mean, what else could it be?"

He touched her hair with the gentlest of caresses. "It could be about love," he said with so much tenderness, her heart tumbled slowly to her tummy.

Now it was her turn to stare. At the beckoning brown of his eyes, at the promise inherent there.

"No," she said, shaking her head. "No. It couldn't be that . . . could it?"

When his mouth tipped into a crooked grin, she knew he'd heard the hope in her voice.

"Why don't you tell me, Katie."

She must have been a little tense, because when the phone rang, she almost connected with the ceiling fan. He snagged her wrist and stayed her when she would have bolted to get it.

"Let your machine pick it up. I want an answer, Katie. Could it be love?"

It could, it could, it could! some insane voice cried inside her. Her mouth had yet to form the words, though, when her recorded message took over.

If you're calling for pizza, you missed it by a digit. If you're calling for Katie, you missed me too. Please leave a message at the beep and I'll get back to you. Sorry, I don't do take-out.

She stared at the phone, stalling for time, praying it was Rachael and she'd have an excuse to run over and pick it up before she rang off. Praying, even, that it might be her mother with her weekly Are-you-taking-care-of-yourself-and-wearing-clean-panties call. It was neither.

"There's something else you don't do, sister," a sinister voice rasped into the machine. "And that's pay attention when someone issues you a friendly warning. The next one won't be so friendly."

As abruptly as the message started, it was over. The harsh click of a broken connection and the serrated buzz of a dial tone filled the suddenly quiet room.

Beside her, she could feel Matthew's tension.

"What the hell was that about?" he asked.

"Crank call?" she suggested hopefully. "Wrong number?"

"Katie," he warned, his eyes darkening to an unrelenting shade of don't-even-think-about-lying-to-me brown.

This time, when she rose, he let her go. Hugging her arms around her middle, she paced to the far side of the living room, then back again to face him.

His expression told her he'd already figured it out. He was not a happy camper.

"That was one of Jim Brackman's thugs, wasn't it?"

Her face must have relayed the accuracy of his conclusion.

He pushed himself off the sofa. "Dammit, Katie, I told you to back away from that mess," he said angrily. Only there was more than anger in his voice. There was worry and hurt and concern. She could see it in his eyes too. Feel it in her bones.

"Let's hear it," he demanded. "All of it."

She knew better than to hedge. But that didn't mean she couldn't downplay it just a bit. "There isn't all that much to tell. Since I started the Brackman investigation, there have been calls to my editor with

IT'S EASY TO ENTER THE
WINNERS CLASSIC SWEEPSTAKES!
PRESENTED BY LOVESWEPT

Where will Passion lead you?

| CARIBBEAN | EUROPE | HAWAII |

YOU'RE INVITED

to enter our Winners Classic Sweepstakes presented by Loveswept for a chance to win a romantic 14-day vacation for two to Hawaii, Europe or the Caribbean ...PLUS $5,000 CASH!

Don't break our heart!

Peel off both halves of this heart and unite them on the Entry Form enclosed. Use both halves to get the most from this special offer.

FREE ENTRY! **FREE BOOKS!**

SPECIAL BONUS:

Get 6 FREE Loveswept books, *plus* another wonderful gift just for trying Loveswept Romances. See details inside...

WIN THE ROMANTIC VACATION OF A LIFETIME...
PLUS $5000 SPENDING MONEY!

Take your pick — Hawaii, Europe or the Caribbean — and enjoy 14 passion-filled days and sultry nights if you're the winner of the Winners Classic Sweepstakes presented by Loveswept. It's *free* to enter, so don't miss out!

YOU COULD WIN YOUR DREAM TRIP!

Just peel off the FREE ENTRY side of our bright red heart, and place it on the Entry Form to the right. But don't stop there!

...AND GET LOVESWEPT EVERY MONTH!

Use the FREE BOOKS sticker, and you'll get your first shipment of 6 Loveswept Romance books absolutely free! PLUS, we'll sign you up for the most romantic book service in the world! About once a month you get 6 new Loveswept novels. You always get 15 days to examine the books, and if you decide to keep them, you'll get 6 books for the price of 4! Be the first to thrill to these new stories. Your Loveswept books will always arrive before they're available in any store. There's no minimum. You can cancel at any time by simply writing "cancel" on your invoice and returning the books to us. We'll pay the postage. So try the Loveswept romantic book service today!

Get a FREE lighted makeup case and 6 free Loveswept books!

Open the tortoise-shell finish case and the mirror lights up! Comes with a choice of brushes for lips, eyes and cheek blusher.

BOTH GIFTS ARE YOURS TO KEEP NO MATTER WHAT!

DON'T HOLD BACK!

1. **No obligation!** No purchase necessary! Enter our Sweepstakes for a chance to win!
2. **FREE!** Get your first shipment of 6 Loveswept books, *and* a lighted makeup case as a free gift.
3. **Save money!** Become a member and about once a month you get 6 books for the price of 4! Return any shipment you don't want.
4. **Be the first!** You'll always receive your Loveswept books before they are available in stores. You'll be the first to thrill to these exciting new stories.

Detach here and mail today.

WINNERS CLASSIC SWEEPSTAKES
Entry Form

YES! I want to see where passion will lead me!

Place
FREE
ENTRY
Sticker
Here

Place
FREE
BOOKS
Sticker
Here

Enter me in the sweepstakes! I have placed my **FREE ENTRY** sticker on the heart.

Send me six *free* Loveswept novels *and* my *free* lighted makeup case! I have placed my **FREE BOOKS** sticker on the heart.

Mend a broken heart. Use both stickers to get the most from this special offer!

61234

NAME_____

ADDRESS_____ APT._____

CITY_____

STATE_____ ZIP_____

Loveswept's Heartfelt Promise to You!

There's no purchase necessary to enter the sweepstakes. There is no obligation to buy when you send for your 6 free books and free lighted makeup case. You may preview each new shipment for 15 days risk-free. If you decide against it, simply return the shipment within 15 days and owe nothing. If you keep the books, pay only $2.25 per book – a savings of $1.25 per book (plus postage & handling, and sales tax in NY and Canada). Prices subject to change. Orders subject to approval. See complete sweepstakes rules at the back of this book.

CD123

Give in to love and see where passion leads you!
Enter the Winners Classic Sweepstakes and
send for your FREE lighted makeup case and
6 FREE Loveswept books today!

(See details inside.)

Detach here and mail today.

BUSINESS REPLY MAIL
FIRST-CLASS MAIL   PERMIT NO. 2456   HICKSVILLE, NY

POSTAGE WILL BE PAID BY ADDRESSEE

Loveswept

Bantam Doubleday Dell Direct, Inc.
PO Box 985
Hicksville NY 11802-9827

NO POSTAGE
NECESSARY
IF MAILED
IN THE
UNITED STATES

complaints about my work, suggestions that they could influence certain big accounts to pull their ads if they didn't get rid of me. Margaret didn't buy it, so nothing was hurt."

"What else?"

He was wound tighter than a treble-string on a steel guitar and tuned just as sharply to her mind's workings. It wouldn't do any good to lie to him. She shrugged and tried for throwaway concern. "I've received some mail. You know, those cute little numbers where they cut out magazine words and paste them on plain white paper? I mean, really, anyone *that* unimaginative can't be taken seriously."

"I want to see them."

His tone left no margin for negotiating. She dug into her desk drawer, found the notes, and tossed them on the coffee table. He read them in clench-jawed silence.

"Matthew, they're bluffing. Grown men playing at good guys and bad guys."

He glared at her. "These guys don't 'play' at anything, Katie. They are dead serious. And they *don't* go by the book."

Hugging her arms tight around herself again, she thought of the menace she'd heard in the voice on her answering machine. She shivered, then realized Matthew had caught her at it.

"I doubt if that character on the phone has ever *read*

a book," she said, trying one of her guileless smiles on Matthew. It didn't wash.

"Back away from this, Katie."

She gnawed on her bottom lip, considering. "Maybe . . ." She hesitated for effect, then let out a martyred sigh. "Maybe you're right. Maybe I am in over my head on this one." She shrugged, conceding defeat. "Maybe I should consider this case closed."

He eyed her warily as he gathered the notes and tucked them into his hip pocket. "Why do I get the feeling you're spoon-feeding me what I want to hear just to placate me?"

She smiled sweetly, skirted his angry bulk, and headed for the kitchen. "Coffee?"

He scowled as she walked by. "Black. And may heaven help you if I find out you crossed me."

"My, my," she said, fluttering her lashes. "Two threats in one night. What's a girl to do?"

What a girl did was plead an upset stomach and send him on his way a short time later. It didn't take much to convince him, given the pig she'd made of herself at the game that afternoon. It took an extreme amount of willpower, however, to make herself let him go. Especially when he picked up their "conversation" where he'd left off that morning.

The man had a way with words. And hands. And hips.

He must have recognized her confusion—maybe it was the dazed look in her eyes when he finally let her go—and the fact that she was struggling with a bad case of too much too soon. Too many revelations. Too many complications.

He was talking about love. He was talking about commitment. She was determined to talk about neither.

And then there was the charm school dropout who'd left such an eloquent message on her answering machine.

"What do you think?" she asked her editor the next morning as she played back the tape for her. They both listened hard to make the words out above the other activities in the busy office.

Margaret Cleary's dark eyes sparkled with a sense of adventure as she tapped a long fingernail against the bow of her designer glasses. "I think, O supersleuth of the decade, that you've dug up some dog's favorite bone and it's shaking the wag right out of his tail."

Katie grinned in spite of herself. When Margaret was excited about something, she lapsed into analogies. Dog analogies were her forte, reserved for her favorite projects. Evidently, the Jim Brackman investigation had hit her top-ten list.

"Who all have you talked with about this, Katie?"

Briefly, Katie outlined her contacts, which included a number of Brackman's competitors, several trips down to city hall to check out building codes and issuance of permits, and an over-cocktails fishing expedition she'd chartered in the hopes of baiting one of Brackman's secretaries into spilling a few worms out of the can.

Margaret's chiding grin clearly suggested Katie leave the analogies to her.

Undaunted, Katie continued. "I got the feeling the secretary was hired more for her, shall we say, coffee-making abilities than for her brain-cell count. Poor thing really wasn't too bright. But then, as close as I could figure, Brackman keeps most of his people in the dark. Per the secretary, he has a lot of behind-closed-doors and out-of-the-office meetings. She did remember seeing Councilman Stein slip out the side door a month or two ago."

Margaret flattened her palms on her desk. "Stein? Did you say Stein?"

Katie nodded.

Margaret snagged a pencil and began chewing on it, a sure sign she was about to blow from the excitement. "Was she sure about it being Stein?"

"Yes. She remembered him from his reelection campaign picture in the paper. You figure there might be some significance to Stein meeting with Brackman?"

"Does a junkyard dog wear a spiked collar?" Margaret flipped the pencil over her shoulder and shot to her feet. "I've been trying to get into that old canine's kennel for years."

"These doggie digs are really fun, Margaret, but can you give me a clue here?"

"Kickbacks, deary. I've suspected for some time that Stein was using his position on the city council to scratch his own—excuse me, to fill his own plate, pad his own wallet, shiver his own timbers, oil his own gears." She added a whoop that did little to diminish the effect of sixty years of purebred sophistication. "Wow! If he and Brackman are having secret meetings, it's a sure bet they're in cahoots on some of these contracts. Don't you see? Brackman greases Stein's palm to make sure he gets the juiciest contracts, and Stein looks the other way when Brackman uses inferior materials to increase his profits."

"Oh my." Katie cupped her palm around the back of her neck and rubbed at a knot that was developing there. "This gets more complicated by the minute."

"And juicer. And more dangerous," Margaret added, eyeing Katie worriedly. "Say the word and I'll put Burnett on this. He's big, he's tough, and if these guys get rough, he's already so ugly that if they mess him up a bit, it won't make much difference."

"I heard that," Cal Burnett mumbled from his corner of the room. "And my wife likes my face just fine the way it is, thank you very much. I won't do it. Not for you, Margaret. But for you, Katie, anything."

Speaking of dogs, Cal was a pug-faced puppy dog hidden in a Saint Bernard costume. He and Katie had worked many a late night together on one project or another. And contrary to every protest he issued, he'd move heaven and earth for Margaret Cleary.

Katie grinned. "Thanks, big guy, but I'm in through the ninth inning on this one."

"Then go for it," Margaret said when a quick look in Cal's direction assured her he'd keep an eye on Katie. "Just be careful."

As Katie settled in behind her desk, she told herself she didn't have to feel guilty where Matthew was concerned. She hadn't lied to him. Not really. She'd just agreed that he was right. And he was right. But she wasn't about to back away from the biggest story she'd ever uncovered just because she was swimming in a little deep water.

It was a simple case of what Matthew didn't know wouldn't hurt him. It wouldn't hurt her either. She knew her job, and she knew how to conduct an investigation. The first order of business was to back off. Let the ripples smooth on the water. Let Brackman and Stein think she'd heeded their warning and was dropping her investigation. Then, slowly but steadily, like a hound hunting a fox, she'd pick up the scent again. She smiled to herself, figuring Margaret would like that one.

She'd be discreet, decisive, and before her quarry

knew they were being tracked again, she'd have them snared. And Matthew, bless his overprotective heart, need never know a thing about it.

Matthew. She looked up from her desk and stared out the fourth-floor office window. She still didn't know what she was going to do about him. One of them had to employ some common sense about their relationship, or nonrelationship, as she insisted it must be. If it couldn't be him, it would have to be her.

Matthew had finally figured out what he was going to do about Katie. He was going to corner her. She did things and said things she didn't want to do or say when she felt boxed in. The truth came out then. Whether in words or in actions, her response to his kisses was sheer unencumbered truth.

She wanted him. She loved him. She was still having difficulty, however, believing he cared for her in more than the physical sense. Haywire hormones, his aching AstroTurf. He'd show her . . . if he could work around said hormones long enough to convince her it was her sweet quirky soul he loved as well as the body it was housed in.

The trouble was, now that he'd admitted to himself that he loved her, he couldn't be around her anymore without wanting to take her to bed. Who was he trying to kid? He'd *never* been able to be around her without wanting to take her to bed.

It occurred to him then that if they could get this hormone stuff out of the way, maybe they could move on to the heart of the matter—*his* heart and how it felt about hers.

Warming to the idea, but knowing he had a few blockades to dodge first, he came up with a plan.

Monday evening he brought her a bottle of wine and a loaf of bread. He answered her suspicious frown with an innocent smile and told her the "thou" would come later. Then he kissed her until they were both wobbly and strolled back home.

Tuesday he brought her flowers. Wildflowers. She stared at them, then at him. He left without a word or the kiss he knew she wanted.

Wednesday he gave her a certificate for a free oil change and a tank of gas. That one really threw her. She scratched her head, opened her mouth, then shut it again. She was still standing in her open doorway when he smugly closed his own door behind him.

Thursday he slid a note under her door. "Tomorrow night. Eight o'clock. I'll bring the chessboard."

"A chessboard?" she said by way of greeting, when he appeared at her front door at precisely eight the next evening.

"Hello to you, too, sweetheart," he said, and dropped a kiss on her sexily pouting lips. "Don't you look pretty?"

What she looked was gorgeous. She'd left her hair

down with the exception of one side, which she'd pulled back with a shell comb and fastened behind her left ear. Exotic-looking earrings that matched the comb dangled and tangled with her sassy curls, brushing the sides of her neck provocatively with every move of her head. Her peasant blouse was a pale peach color. The off-the-shoulder style was as flirty and feminine as the full, gauzy pastel-print skirt that hit her legs about mid-calf and his libido dead center.

And the scent of sweet clover that clung to her skin and filled the air around her made him ache to taste each honey-colored inch of her.

"You've got a lot of nerve, Spencer. You've given me wine, given me flowers, given me oil, given me gas—" She snapped her mouth shut, cleared her throat delicately, and forged ahead. "And now you show up here wanting to play chess. If this is your idea of a seduction, I've got to tell you, you started out like gangbusters, but you're sliding downhill fast."

He knew then his strategy had worked. He'd thrown her totally and completely for a loop. She felt both curious and cornered, or she never in a million mutterings would have mentioned the word seduction . . . or dressed as though she were anticipating one. Obviously, the thought had been on her mind as much as it had been on his.

"Seduction?" he asked, all innocence and light. "Did you want me to seduce you, Katie?"

She was so cute, trying to look huffy. She couldn't quite hold on to it, though. She was melting, just a little. He could see it in her eyes, hear it in her sigh, before she stiffened and lifted her stubborn little chin.

"What I want," she said, "is for you to get your head back on straight and think about what you might be giving up by getting involved with me."

"What I'd be giving up? Are you referring to the long, lonely nights or the emptiness crowding my days?"

Her eyes beseeched him. "Joey," she said simply. "You could be giving up Joey."

He touched a hand to her hair, loving her more by the minute. "Never, baby. Never him. Not again. And never you. I've just found you."

Her eyes were glistening as she turned away.

"You let me worry about the situation with Joey, okay?" He walked up behind her and wrapped his arms around her, tugging her back against him. "Trust me, Katie. I won't let it be a problem."

Sighing again, she leaned into his embrace. "You're making a mistake."

"I'm done making mistakes."

"Oh, yeah?" The way she sagged trustingly against him told him she was weakening. "If that's the case, then why is there a chessboard pressed against my tummy instead of—" She gasped when he nudged her from behind with his hips.

"Instead of this?" he asked, too happy and too hot

and too bothered to pull away and hide the evidence of his desire for her.

"You are the darnedest man," she muttered, but he heard the laughter and longing mixed with her exasperation.

Gripping her by her shoulders, he turned her in his arms. "Chess, I've found," he said as he kissed her, once on the lips, once on her nose, once on each fluttering eyelid, "is the great get-acquainter."

She looped her arms around his neck. "Acquainter? Is that a word?"

"We're playing chess, sweetheart, not Scrabble, and you can learn a lot about a person over a chessboard. I intend to learn a lot about you tonight, Katie." The message he relayed with his eyes was unmistakable.

She shivered with sudden awareness. It was a slow, sensual shimmy that began with a subtle shifting of her shoulders and ended with a discernible quaking of her knees.

"Why don't you get the wine?" he suggested, nipping her ear. Because he couldn't not do it, he tasted the delicate skin behind it.

She sighed dreamily. "Okay."

"Katie?" he said after a long moment.

"Hmm?"

"Tonight would be nice."

"Tonight?"

"The wine? Tonight?" He pried her arms from around his neck and searched her face. "You're taking all the challenge out of this, you know. I'd really planned that loosening you up would be my project for the night."

"I was supposed to play hard to get?"

He smiled. "You were supposed to be confused, and uncertain, and even a little frightened about your feelings for me and where those feelings might lead us."

After a long look, she tore her gaze away. She stared at a spot beyond his shoulder, then down at the floor between their feet. "Then—then you won't be disappointed if I told you that I am confused . . . and uncertain . . . and scared down to my sandals about my feelings for you and where they might lead us?"

Such a brave girl, he thought. Such a vulnerable, lost little soul. What happened to you, Katie, he wanted to know, that made you so afraid to give in to love?

"No," he said, threading his fingers through the hair at her temple and cupping her head in his palm. "I won't be disappointed." He dropped a kiss on her forehead. "Now, how about that wine?"

How, Katie blasted herself mentally as she screwed the devil out of the cork, had she let this happen? Would she never learn?

What had happened to all those self-sacrificing, noble *You're going to stay out of his and Joey's life* speeches she'd suffered through alone each night in her bed? What had happened to the *Your road's only wide enough for one* concept? Or, her favorite, *Sex isn't worth the hassle and love isn't in the budget. The investment's too steep.*

She was such a fraud. Such a faker.

And he—he was such a man.

She shivered just thinking about what the night might have in store if she'd only let things happen. Live for the moment, right? Wasn't that how it was done these days?

And hadn't she tried? She'd repeatedly warned him off. It wasn't her fault he wasn't listening. He soon would be, though. Men never stuck around her for long. Even Matthew, with his kind and gentle heart, wouldn't have it in him to put up with her silliness. Sooner or later, it would get to him, just as it had with every other man she'd given her trust.

Filling a tray with two glasses and the wine, she headed toward the living room. Whether she decided to send him home or keep him for the night was still up for grabs.

Maybe she was worrying over nothing. After all, they were only talking about playing chess. Right. And Elvis was alive and well and living in her refrigerator next to the jelly donuts.

When she didn't find the chessboard set up on her coffee table or Matthew anywhere in the room, she followed the sound of the music. It led her to her bedroom.

The first thing she noticed was his shoes on the floor beside the bed. The second thing was the song playing on the radio. The Doors again.

The sequence of discovery got a bit muzzy after that, when she spotted the chessboard set up in the middle of her bed and Matthew stretched out on his side, his head propped in his palm as he diligently positioned the pieces.

Chess, my eye, she thought, smiling in spite of herself.

And then she just stopped and enjoyed the view. She hadn't yet gotten used to the effect he had on her every time she saw him. All that sleek, toned muscle made her think of satin wrapped around steel. The words "whip-cord" and "lean" and "man" and "machine" got all tangled up with the visual picture of him filling up her bed. He looked quite wonderful there. And he was so beautiful, she forgave him his lack of subtlety.

He looked up and smiled when he saw her in the doorway.

She raised her eyebrows in return.

He gave her a one-shouldered shrug and a choirboy grin. "I learned to play on my bed in my dorm room," he said by way of explanation. "Still plan my best strategy stretched out across a box spring."

Two, she decided, could play this game. "We still talking about chess?"

His eyes danced as he resumed his study of the board. "Do you play?"

"I repeat, are we still talking about chess?"

"It's a great game."

She set the tray on the nightstand and poured them each a glass of wine. "Some say it's overrated."

"You've used that term before—about other things." Looking up at her, he patted the mattress on the opposite side of the board. "Come on. Let's see what I can do to change your mind."

It was the implied promise that finally convinced her. She hesitated for only a moment before toeing off her sandals, easing onto her side, and propping herself up on an elbow across from him. The scoop neck of her peasant blouse slipped lower. In for a penny, in for a pound, she decided, and in a move she considered daring, she left it there.

Hoping against hope that he wouldn't see or hear the pounding of her heart, she picked up a chess piece and asked, "So . . . what are these little bullet guys for?"

He plucked the pawn out of her hand and replaced it on the board. "They're called pawns and their basic purpose is to sacrifice to give the other pieces better position."

"Position?" She swallowed some wine.

"Position." The eyes that met hers over the rim of her wineglass were full of innuendo. His gaze then lazily cataloged the slope of her bare shoulder, the indentation of her waist, the flare of her hip. "Much of the intrigue of the game is based on position."

His words said so much, she mused. More than met the ear. And his eyes said so much more. Right now they were trained on her mouth. And they were smoldering.

"And these?" she asked, picking up another piece with trembling fingers. "What do these little horsey guys do?"

"These little horsey guys," he said, "are called knights. They protect the king. Along with the bishops."

"Bishops?"

"The little pointy-headed guys," he said, reverting to her language as he showed her which piece. "And these are called rooks or castles. Each piece has a different mode of transportation around the board."

"And the queen," she asked quietly, fingering the intricately carved piece. "Who protects her?"

"All the king's horses and all the king's men."

Couldn't put Katie together again, she finished silently. She wanted so badly for this to be good and was so afraid that it wouldn't be. When he caught her hand in his and brought it to his mouth, dread quickly shifted to anticipation.

She'd always been fascinated by his eyes, but never more than now. They held her motionless, telling her it was all right, that it would be so good, before his thick, sun-kissed lashes dropped to hide the heat.

Opening her palm, he lightly bit the heel of her hand. A sensation laboring somewhere between fever and chill eddied down her spine. A delicious pressure alien and new and exceedingly erotic tightened in her belly, when he turned his face into her palm and scraped the slight stubble of his five-o'clock shadow against her skin.

As always with Matthew, it was too much. He made her feel too much. Too much hunger. Too much heat. Too much wanting. The panic grabbed her hard and low.

Her eyes must have betrayed her anxiety, for he released her hand.

"The thing about chess," he said so slowly and carefully that she knew he wasn't talking about chess but about them and what was about to happen, "is that everyone plays at a different pace."

"Pace?" she squeaked as she felt the pace of her heart gear up to set a new land-speed record.

"Um-hum. Pace and strategy," he continued in that same slow, reassuring cadence. "You can take all the time you want to calculate your first move, and then your next. Or you can just dive right in and take a chance you'll throw the other player off guard with a little recklessness."

She wished she could be reckless. Reckless and daring and all the things a man like Matthew needed from a woman. For him, she was determined to try.

"And how . . ." She stopped, then in what she felt was essentially another bold maneuver, asked him point-blank, "How do *you* approach the game?"

"With patience, Katie." The look in his eyes backed up his statement. "I'd never push or prod or badger you into making a move before you were ready. Does that work for you?"

She chewed on her lip for a moment, then made her decision. She knew it wasn't right, but she wanted to be with this man. She wanted to feel his heat, feel his hunger, feel the need in him wrap around her and in the process, fulfill her own.

When she met his eyes again, she saw he'd been watching her. If she hadn't realized it before, she knew in that moment just how much he wanted her. A stunning mixture of anticipation and sensual hunger flashed across his face. And something else. Something she wanted to believe in but just couldn't let herself. It wasn't love she saw in his eyes. It couldn't be love. Not from a man like him. Not for someone like her.

No, it wasn't love, but she suspected that he

thought it was. And that thought counted . . . enough for her to trust him with a heart she knew he would never intentionally break.

Picking up a pawn from the center of the board, she drew a deep breath and handed over that trust. "Show me what to do."

SEVEN

She put his king in check with her fourth move.

Matthew scratched his jaw, studied the board, and tried to decide if she was beating him by sheer dumb luck, his own lack of concentration, or if she was scamming him.

"Did I do something wrong?" she asked.

He squinted up at her, then back to the board, searching for a way to save his king and his face at the same time. After careful deliberation he made his move.

In what appeared to be a totally throwaway decision on her part, she countered with her bishop.

"Was that okay?" she asked, all wide-eyed quest for approval as she searched his face, which he knew was set in an expression of acute shock. She'd just beaten him—and in less than ten minutes.

"That move you made resulted in checkmate," he said tightly, "and yes, that's okay—from your point of view."

"It means I won?"

He studied the board again in disbelief. When he felt the bed begin to shake with her attempt to quell her laughter, he didn't have to look up into those big, scampering eyes of hers to know the little hellion had bamboozled him.

"You're laughing now," he said as he calmly relieved her of her wineglass, setting both it and his on the nightstand. Sweeping the chessboard, pieces and all, onto the floor, he dove for her. "Let's see if you're still laughing five minutes from now."

"If you . . . if you could have seen your face," she said between giggles as he lay spread-eagle across her and pinned her hands above her head.

"The penalties for toying with my good intentions are severe," he said with studied menace. "And I think I'm going to derive intense personal satisfaction in imposing every one. One for laughing, one for scamming me, one for bruising my fragile male ego, and one, I think, to teach you a lesson."

"Oh, good." She squirmed in anticipation beneath him. "Another lesson."

"You're not paying attention, you little hustler. You're supposed to feel threatened."

Her eyes grew wide with subservience and mirth. "Oh, I do. I do."

"Yeah, well, it would be a lot more convincing if you'd quit laughing."

"I'm sorry. Really. I'm sorry. I'll stop. There. See? Not laughing anymore."

He gave up and dropped his head on the comforter beside her cheek, when she dissolved into another fit of giggles.

"'What do these little horsey guys do?'" he mimicked, then groaned at his own gullibility. "What a sap. I should have known right then you were taking me for a ride."

"Don't take it so hard," she soothed, managing finally to get herself under control. "I was raised playing the game. The McDonalds of Jasper County are known for their talents at chess. Besides, you were trying so hard to be sensitive and patient with me, I didn't have the heart to tell you."

"Sensitive, patient . . . gullible. That's me." He sighed tiredly.

The laughter in her eyes gave way to tenderness. She tugged her hands out of his and cupped his face. "All of the above," she said softly. "As well as gentle and kind."

"You make me sound like a basset hound."

She smiled. "And virile, brave, handsome . . ."

He puffed up a little, just for show. "Throw in sexy

son-of-a-gun and you'll have made giant strides toward atoning for your underhanded ways."

She toyed with a button on his shirt. "Maybe I'd like to hear what the penalties are first . . . before you forgive me completely, that is, and make it too easy on me."

"Ah, yes, the penalties," he said, considering this bolder, more confident side of her. Shifting his weight, he eased a knee experimentally between her thighs. When she made room for him there, he pressed the issue. "Certain penalties can be . . . intimidating. Take, for example, the penalty for laughing. It could be very, veeerrry stiff." He pressed his hips and hers deeper into the mattress to illustrate his point.

"Yes," she said, her voice a breathless shiver. "I—I, ah, get the distinct impression that it might be."

He got the distinct impression that was just fine with her. It might have been the way she sighed, with that desperate little catch in her breath, or the way she raised her leg and rubbed it against his hip.

"As for scamming me . . ." He watched her face flush as he hooked a finger under the scoop neck of her blouse and tugged it down slowly. "Now that particular penalty might take some thought. For instance," he continued, lowering his mouth to the skin he'd just bared and had been waiting to taste for so long, "I might decide you deserve a good, thorough tongue-lashing for that specific transgression."

Again she rewarded him with that sexy shiver of anticipation. "Tongue-lashing?"

"I'll demonstrate."

Nudging the blouse lower with his nose, he did a little shivering of his own when his actions revealed the curve of her pert breast, the tight thrust of its berry-pink tip. Lowering his head, he proceeded to give her a generous sampling of the treatment he had in mind.

"Oh . . ." She sighed and stretched and arched into his mouth as he strafed her nipple with his tongue. "I—I can see where . . . that would be most . . . effective."

Apparently, it was more than effective. Her throaty moan was a dead giveaway that he was torturing her into delirium. The fists knotted in his hair and drawing him closer were telling too.

So was the difficulty he was having breathing . . . and thinking about anything but burying himself inside all that silky, restless heat. She was like a sizzling skillet beneath him. Her skin, honey-sweet and sunburn-hot, fostered myriad demands that surged like lightning through his lower body. He couldn't get enough of her. Couldn't get close enough.

"And as for the bruise you gave to my ego," he managed to whisper against the fire that was her flesh, "I'll let you choose the best penalty for that. But whatever you decide, please, sweetheart, make it fast. I think I'm about to explode here."

If there had ever been hesitancy on her part, if there had ever been uncertainty, both were forgotten in that instant. She wasn't the least bit hesitant when she wrenched his shirt open and stripped if off his shoulders. She wasn't at all uncertain when she reached between them and yanked down his zipper.

What she was, was all woman. The kind of woman he'd known she would become for him. Wild, wanton, wanting. And what she wanted was him. He gloried in the knowledge and in the need he recognized from the pace she set.

Caught up in her unbridled urgency, struggling to contain his own, he shucked his jeans and shorts. Rolling to his knees, he pulled her up with him.

Hungry to see, and taste, and feel everything that made her Katie, he swept his gaze from her wildly tousled hair and flushed cheeks to the blouse draped provocatively low on her breasts, then down to the yards of skirt tangled about her knees. "I don't want to tear it," he whispered, but the gruffness in his voice and the harshness of his breathing warned her that he'd rip it to shreds if he had to. "So please, sweetheart . . . figure out the fastest way to get out of those clothes."

A look so shy and vulnerable, yet so proudly sexy, sparkled in her eyes as she answered his command by stripping the blouse to her waist.

She was working frantically at her braided-rope belt when he reached for her. He couldn't help it. He pulled her to him. His hands looked big and dark and erotically commanding as they encircled the pale skin and fragile framework of her ribs. Bending to her breast, he sucked her deeply into his mouth. She gasped in surprise, then moaned in pure pleasure before a groan of frustration escaped.

"Matthew," she pleaded when her fingers failed to master the knot at her waist. "Help me!"

With great reluctance, he released her and attacked the belt himself. "You'd have made a great boy scout," he muttered darkly when he met with no more success than she had.

"Boy scout?" she wailed, raking the hair out of her eyes.

He sat back on his heels, and in spite of the hassle and the heat and the frustration sizzling her eyes to a combatant cobalt, he smiled at her. Lord, she was a beautiful sight.

She was tangled and mussed, rosy and pink where he'd loved her, evocatively seductive as her bare breasts heaved with every agitated breath she drew . . . and she was damn near ready to deck him.

"Relax, sweetheart, I was referring to your expert knot, not the package it's wrapping."

With a suppressed groan, she pressed her fists against the part of her that longed to become one with him. "Hurry!"

That did it.

"The hell with the damn knot," he growled, reaching for her again. He tossed her to her back, shoved her skirts to her waist, and tugged off her lacy panties in one smooth, precise move. There wasn't a trace of the choirboy in his grin as he dangled the panties above his head before giving them a victory fling across the room.

"My hero," she crooned, making room for him as he settled between her thighs.

"My woman," he answered as he sank slowly into her.

In that moment when flesh blended to flesh and startled blue eyes met exultant brown, the panic, the playing, the urgency ceased to matter. All that mattered was the longing. And the loving. And the love.

He watched her face as he moved inside her. Watched her eyes cloud over with mindless, wondrous pleasure. Watched the sigh leave her lips, the flush of desire paint her cheeks, and the last thread of inhibition unravel from her slender body like so much mist trailing a rapidly shooting star.

"Oh, Katie." He kissed her, seeking her surrender, knowing he was negotiating his own. "It's . . . so . . . good."

"Yes," she whispered, sounding surprised and awed and aware of her power as a woman as she drew him into another deep, drugging kiss. "Yes."

He lost himself then. In the slow, steady rhythm

they set together. In the complete sense of homecoming. In her throaty sighs and sultry whispers.

One moment he was floating, the next skyrocketing. When she cried his name and began convulsing around him like a fragile, feminine fist, he was right with her. He exploded inside her with a final surge that set him careening over the edge and into a night that was still . . . sheets that were hot . . . and a woman who was totally his.

But for the moon winking through the chintz curtains that fluttered at her bedroom window, the room was completely dark. The mist of passion still shimmered on their skin when Matthew turned on the light so he could seek her face.

They'd long ago managed to get her out of her skirt and toss it, along with a pesky pawn, out of the bed. Her hair, a beautiful tangle of golden silk, framed a face as multifaceted as a diamond and just as beautiful. She looked thoroughly sated, completely loved. But as he watched her grow increasingly uncomfortable with his scrutiny, he saw the uncertainty creep back in.

"You okay?" he asked, tracing a finger along a trickle of perspiration that trailed through the gentle valley between her breasts.

She expelled a shuddering sigh. "I don't think I'll ever see 98.6 again."

He smiled and kissed her swollen lips. "It did get a little hot, didn't it?" He whispered another kiss against the damp skin at her temple. "Still think it's over-rated?"

Her smile was lazy and teasing as she repeated a question that had gotten lost much earlier amid tangled sheets and restless hunger. "We still talking about chess?"

"You know what I'm talking about," he said, giving her earlobe a playful nip.

"Hmm. I guess I do. And I just might have to adjust my rating system."

"Yeah? I thought that might be the case when I had to remind you to breathe."

She was even prettier when she blushed. Everything from her cheeks to her breasts turned a delicate pink that made him think of wild roses.

"You were, ah, very good with . . . instructions."

He raised up on an elbow so he could see her face. "And you're a very good responder."

"Obviously. I mean, I must have breathed when you told me to or we wouldn't be having this conversation."

He mulled that over for a moment before realizing what this conversation was really all about. She was second-guessing herself. Her desirability. Her ability to please him. Her importance in his life.

He didn't want her second-guessing anything.

Watching her eyes, he covered her breast with his hand and kneaded gently. She rewarded him with a sultry shiver. He loved that shiver. And the feel of her. Her slight weight, her silky texture, the velvet softness of her nipple before it tightened and hardened against his palm.

"They're not much, are they?" she said shyly.

Hello. Insecurity knocking. He saw it in her eyes as his gaze searched them. "Ask me if I care."

"Do you?" Her voice was very small, and before she looked away, he saw how much his answer mattered.

Lowering his head to her breast, he loved her with his mouth until she moaned. "Feel good?" he murmured against her skin.

"Ummm-hmm."

"Then that's all I care about." Because he cared about her. He had to make her see that this wasn't just an issue of sex, though Lord knew sex was definitely an issue. It was an issue of life. She was so full of it. She made him want to get his fill of it too.

And it was an issue of love, a subject he was sure she wasn't ready to face. Before he tackled that particular topic, he had to do something about her pencil-thin self-image and the paper-thin ego that went with it.

"Katie?"

"Ummm?"

"Could I interest you in another game of chess?"

❖━━━━━━━━━━━❖

He fell asleep around midnight. After dropping a kiss on his brow, Katie scooted out of bed, found his discarded shirt—minus a few buttons—and slipped into it. It smelled like him, and wrapping it around her gave her the illusion of being held by him.

When she came back from the kitchen, a carton of chocolate ice cream in hand, he was propped up against the headboard, his dark eyes closed, the sheet trailing low on his hips.

She stood there for a long time, the ice cream getting warm, her hand getting cold, the rest of her heating by degrees, and just watched him. Watched him breathe and sigh and lazily stir as the muted light from her bedside lamp cast his face and body in silken shadows.

He was so beautiful. So full of fun and love and laughter. And she was full to bursting with love for him. So much love that it scared her, because she knew when he got wise and left her, she'd have the love to deal with for a long, long time.

She'd thought he was asleep until he murmured her name.

"Katie?"

She grinned, because just seeing him in her bed made her happy. Just hearing him say her name in that lazy, hazy, you're-my-girl kind of way made her heart swell.

"I'm here," she said, and watched him settle himself deeper into the pillows.

"Is it just my imagination, or are you a long ways away?" he asked, never opening his eyes.

The sheet had slipped lower, and, if possible, her heart felt a little fuller. Crazy in love, brazenly in lust, she moved to stand by the bed. "You want to know what I thought the very first time I saw you?"

He stretched and shifted and sank farther into the mattress. "What? What did you think?"

She eased one knee onto the bed. "I thought, I'd like to make love to that man until he's comatose."

One corner of his mouth tipped up as one hand crawled with slow, intimate languor along her thigh. "And what do you think now?"

Smiling at the listless sprawl of his long legs beneath the sheet, the relaxed stretch of his beautifully muscled arms, the deep, even breaths of a man thoroughly spent from making exquisite, passionate love, she trailed her fingertips from his chest to the dark whorling hair on his lean belly. "I think my goal is in sight."

Drowsy heat shot to fiery need when he opened his eyes. He snagged her wrist and pulled her across him until she straddled his hips.

"Think again, sweet cheeks," he advised on a husky whisper. "There's life in this body yet . . . and you're just the woman to resurrect it. Besides, you know what they say." Reaching for his shirt, he slid it slowly off her shoulders. "A goal worth pursuing is a goal worth working for."

"They do say that, don't they?" she said, settling her bottom more intimately onto his lap.

He sucked in a harsh breath and watched her through eyes grown dark with passion. "Did you have anything in particular in mind for that ice cream or were you just going to let it melt all over the bed?"

She made sure she had his full attention before answering. "I thought I'd let it melt all over you."

He swallowed hard. "A waste of good chocolate."

The reaction she felt against her bare bottom, however, expressed a different opinion entirely.

"I hadn't exactly planned on letting it go to waste." The huskiness in her voice was provoked by anticipation as his hands, spread wide and possessively over her thighs, stroked up and down and up again, stalling at the spot where feminine curls met masculine need.

He reacted to the smoke in her eyes with a strangled groan. "Lucky for you, I'm in an indulgent mood."

"Umm," she said, digging into the ice cream with her spoon while deciding where to start. "Lucky for me . . ."

He left her bed with great reluctance at six o'clock Saturday morning for a site inspection that couldn't wait but with a promise to be back by six o'clock that evening.

Though she missed him terribly, Katie had a fun day playing Suzie homemaker. It was an illusion, but it was an illusion she treasured and she refused to let anything shatter it.

She baked bread, brushed the dust off the pasta machine Margaret have given her for Christmas the year before, and even fit in a quick trip to Victoria's Secret for a couple of pieces of lingerie that were guaranteed to make him forget that she'd burned the bread and scorched the pasta.

It was his own fault. She couldn't concentrate on anything so mundane as food when she had her memories of last night to distract her . . . not to mention her anticipation at being with him again that night.

She wondered if a person could die from too much sex and figured if she survived the rest of the weekend, she'd have her answer. If she died, she'd die a happy woman. If she lived, she'd continue her quest for knowledge at every opportunity. And next week was soon enough to think about the future.

Good to his word, Matthew arrived at exactly six o'clock. Freshly showered, cleanly shaved, and tucked neatly into a pair of cutoffs and a brand new T-shirt with the message I WILL FOR CHOCOLATE scrawled brazenly across his chest, he smiled tiredly at her from the outside of her sliding door.

"Rough day?" she asked sympathetically as she tugged open the door for him.

He slumped into one of her kitchen chairs. "Don't feel so hot."

She was a bit suspicious of the grin lurking under all that melodrama. When he grasped her hand and pressed it to his forehead, she knew she was the one being scammed this go-round.

"Tell Mama what's wrong," she cooed, playing along.

He sighed theatrically. "Headache. I feel cranky. Irritable. A little bloated."

The mischief in his eyes when he snuck a peek at her to see if she was buying his woeful line was just too much.

It took everything in her to stifle a grin. "Got that not-so-fresh feeling', huh?"

His broad shoulders drooped. "Yeah."

"Sounds like PMS to me."

He shook his head and drew her onto his lap. "SRS."

"SRS?" she asked, linking her arms around his neck.

"Sperm Retention Syndrome," he whispered against her lips. "Katie . . . it's been *twelve* hours."

She glanced over his shoulder at the clock. "And five minutes."

Dragging her into a deep, searing kiss, he explored her body so diligently, a doctor would have commended him for his thoroughness. "I missed you like hell."

"Me too," she admitted, doing a little exploring of her own.

"Do you think there's something wrong with us? I mean, you make me feel like a teenager. Do you think we ought to cool the physical part a little before—"

"I think," she interrupted, slipping off his lap and leading him toward the bedroom at a trot, "you ask too many questions."

"But what if—"

She silenced him with a kiss that, when it finally ended, left him blessedly speechless.

Touching her index finger to the center of his chest, she gave a delicate nudge that toppled him backward onto her bed. Then she clambered right on top of him, and the only questions left between them were ones that dealt with buttons and zippers and the rest of the barriers that kept bare skin from pressing against bare skin.

They surfaced for food around eight o'clock. And she'd been right. Watching her flit around the kitchen in a sinfully sheer French silk nightshirt over thong bikini panties, Matthew didn't seem to notice that the bread was a bit crusty and the clam linguini had a distinctive charbroiled flavor.

What he noticed was her. She loved every look, every intimate, heated touch, every love word and every lust word he spoke so freely and so generously.

She didn't even mind when a little later, back in her bedroom, he coaxed her into another chess game—a real one—that he insisted wasn't a grudge match. She let him win. He knew it and rewarded her by letting her pick the next game.

She picked strip poker.

"But I'm already stripped to the skin," he protested when she came at him with a deck of cards in hand.

"Then I guess I win," she cried, shooting the cards across the room.

He rewarded her again until, gasping his name, she begged for release.

He doled it out in slow, exquisitely torturous measures.

"I'm the winner, Katie," he whispered, looking up past the subtle curve of her belly, the gentle swell of her breasts, and into eyes gone smoky with mindless passion. "And you . . ." He lowered his head and lost himself again in her taste and her heat and the wonder that made her so special. "You are the prize."

Cradling her hips in his hands while she trembled and convulsed, then shuddered slowly back to awareness, he pressed deep, tender kisses to the delicate points of her hipbones and to the faint surgical scar that spanned between them.

She had to know by now he was aware of the scar, Matthew mused. The fact that she hadn't talked about it supported his suspicions that it might have everything to do with her reluctance to completely open up to him.

He decided he could wait. He would wait. He told her so without words as he pressed one final kiss to the incision before seeking her mouth with his own and filling her the way he felt filled whenever he was near her.

Trust what you feel, Katie, he urged her with each deep, burning stroke. Believe what you see. In my eyes. In my heart. In my soul.

EIGHT

Katie watched Matthew and Joey through her kitchen window as she stacked a platter with hamburger patties. With bittersweet longing, she battled a niggling awareness of what she'd let happen over the past few weeks.

Was it really so much to ask, she pleaded with her conscience, just to be with them for a while? Just to experience the fun and fullness of Matthew's attention?

Yeah, she answered dismally. It was. And now she had to pay the price for being high on life, high on love, and so dangerously low on common sense.

Although she'd assured herself she had been living only for the moment, she realized now that she'd let herself get in too deep. She'd indulged selfishly. The problem was, she wasn't the only one who was going to get hurt because of it. Her disregard for Matthew and Joey's future together had been reckless and stupid.

Because she'd thought with her heart instead of her head, *they* might end up paying the highest price.

It's up to you to set things right, she lectured herself. And you know how to do it. You curtsy smartly, bid them a fond farewell, and exit, stage left. There. Problem solved—except for one itsy-bitsy factor. She couldn't seem to work up the courage to bow out of their lives.

Soon, she promised herself. Pasting on a happy-sunshine smiling face, she headed out the door to where father and son were waiting by the grill.

"All right!" Joey shouted. "Hammmburrrger-rrsss!"

Joey's enthusiasm prompted Matthew's. "Umm. Yes. Meat!" he uttered in a guttural monotone, and thumped a fist to his chest. "We want meat!"

This set Joey into a spasm of giggles. Marching in a circle around the grill, he joined in on the chant, mimicking his father's antics.

"Hold your grapevine, Tarzan. You too, Boy," Katie said, too weak-willed to do anything but join in on the fun. "Your protein levels don't appear to be in any danger of extinction."

Joey giggled again and made another pass around the grill.

"You might be right about the protein." Matthew's voice dropped to a whisper as he leaned in close and scooped the burgers onto the grate. "But my testosterone level is in dire need of depletion."

"*You* are a terrible flirt," she said, dodging his playful attempt to nibble on her neck.

"And here I thought I was getting pretty good at it."

She rolled her eyes. "Maybe 'outrageous' is the word I was searching for."

"And effective?" he asked, his eyes full of mischief and hope.

"Too effective, I'm afraid." She sobered abruptly, in awe of just how effective he was.

He frowned. Before he could ask her what was wrong, Joey caught his full attention.

"What's tes . . . testos . . . rum?"

Both pairs of adult eyes zeroed in on the little blond boy who wasn't supposed to have heard what he heard.

"I'll leave that one to you, O King of the Jungle."

Hiding a sudden and unexpected threat of tears behind a broad smile, Katie hustled back into her kitchen.

Matthew was a rat, she thought. He'd made it so easy for her to drift along with the fantasy. He didn't pressure. He didn't prod. He just managed to make her feel special and loved, and to include her in his and Joey's plans so easily that it made her question if it was his finesse or her lack of honest protest that made it so simple.

He never actually mentioned the L word. He was too smart for that. He let her know, however, that it was in the back of his mind. His silence on the subject told her he figured she'd bolt like a startled thoroughbred if he spelled out his own feelings or pressured her for an admission. He was right.

So instead of talking about it, he demonstrated how he felt over and over again, with silly romantic gifts, with lingering touches, and with unselfish, uninhibited physical pleasures.

And with the looks that sometimes came over his face when he saw her, like the one she caught now as their gazes met through the window. It was territorial, that look, and tender, and made promises of what he had in mind for her when he got her alone.

Lord, how she loved that man. Too much to cause him to lose the most important thing in his life.

It wasn't enough that she loved the father. She'd also fallen in love with the son. They were in cahoots, those two. She looked forward to Joey's every-other-weekend visits as much as Matthew. And why not? They made it so natural for her to join in on the play, the special bedtime moments she yearned for and cherished, the idea of the three of them becoming a family. "Get used to it" was the implied message.

Well, she'd been getting real used to it. And it had to stop. What Joey needed was stability. What she could offer him was not even a kissin' cousin of the word.

Slipping back outside with the salad, she avoided

Matthew's probing look by mentally trading one problem for another. Brackman.

Things were starting to heat up on that campfire. To date, she'd opened up a Pandora's box of Brackman's transgressions, which crossed the bridge and back again from grossly unethical to patently illegal. As Margaret had suspected, every finger pointed to Councilman Stein and kickbacks in exchange for key contracts. Those contracts were making Brackman and the councilman rich, and were placing the residents of the apartment complexes built with taxpayer's money in imminent danger. They were, in short, slime. And she wanted them. Bad.

She glanced at Matthew and tried to ignore her guilt over withholding her investigation from him. She'd hedged and parried and skirted any direct questions he'd asked her with all the guile of a snake slithering under a rock. For that backhanded deceit, she felt as low as said snake.

Later that night, after they'd tucked Joey into bed, she and Matthew were sitting on his deck, sharing the moonlight, the cool night breeze, and the mellow sounds of KCMO. He startled her by saying without preamble, "It's time you fill me in, Katie."

She didn't have to ask what he was alluding too. The tone of his voice said it all. Still, dancing around the topic of Brackman came as naturally as breathing. "Fill you in?"

He leaned forward in his chair, propped his elbows on his thighs, and clenched his hands together. "I've resigned myself to the fact that nothing I can say to you is going to draw you away from the Brackman investigation." Instead of looking at her, he studied his hands as if he found his strength there before he continued. "It doesn't mean I like it, it just means I've accepted it.

"What I can't accept . . ." He paused and looked up at her then. The hurt and intensity etched on his face stalled her heartbeat. "What I can't accept, Katie, is the knowledge that I'm in the dark about what you're doing. I need to know you're okay. That you've covered all the bases and protected your blind side."

She loved him very much at that moment. More than was prudent. More than she should have allowed and far too much to dodge his questions any longer. "I've been very careful."

His lips thinned, but he nodded. "I'm glad to hear that, but it isn't enough. I've said it every way I can think of and I still haven't convinced you that that man can hurt you." His dark gaze pierced hers. "Katie . . . I don't think I could handle it if you got hurt."

"Matthew." She reached out and covered his hands with hers. "I'm not going to get hurt."

"That's because I'm not going to let you. I want you to let me help you with this one, Katie. Just this one time."

No one had ever wanted to lay himself on the line for her. Just for her. Touched to the point of feeling wounded, she blinked back tears. "I don't want to involve you in this." She didn't have to explain her reasons. Matthew's bid to regain custody of Joey was an ever-present, if unspoken, motive.

"Too late," he said. "I am involved. Just like I'm involved with you. Whether you choose to acknowledge it or not isn't going to make it go away. Now tell me what's going on."

Katie closed her eyes. Tight. She drew in a breath. A big one. When she let it out, opened her eyes, and saw the honest intensity on his face, she gave up. She owed him the truth.

"Okay," she began haltingly. "This is what I've got so far."

He listened in tight-lipped silence while she outlined everything she'd uncovered, right down to the hows and whys and whens. "The only thing we can't pin down is direct participation."

"Explain," he said evenly.

"Brackman's smart. He covers his tracks with middlemen and holding companies. He very quietly lines the pockets of his 'special building inspector,' who turns around and issues false reports while Councilman Stein lurks in the background like the great city savior and touts his ability to bring in government-subsidized projects under cost projections."

"All right. How do you propose to expose them?"

If there had been a trace of skepticism in his tone, she'd have packed it in right then. But there was none. And there was no reprimand.

"That's the kicker. Short of direct confrontation, I'm stumped."

He leaned back in his chair. "I have an idea."

She leaned forward in hers as he began talking. Surprise was her initial reaction. It shouldn't have been. He'd said he was involved and he'd obviously meant it.

Katie gave herself credit. She heard him out before she exploded. "Absolutely, positively, unequivocally no!"

"Could you be a little bit more decisive here?"

"Matthew, this is not a joking matter. I won't let you do it."

"But it could work."

"And if it didn't? You could end up in jail yourself if it backfired. Or worse. You could end up hurt. I will not, under any circumstances, let you dangle yourself as bait under the crooked councilman's nose. I will not let you compromise yourself to draw him into what he thinks is another kickback scheme."

She bounced out of her chair and paced the deck before swinging around to face him with more arguments. "Matthew, if he caught on to you and it didn't play out, he could have you arrested. Paint you as the blackest of blackguards since Bluebeard. It could ruin your business, not to mention totally obliterate your chance of getting Joey back. My Lord, if the Handcocks got wind that you were foolhardy enough to even *think* about initiating an entrapment scheme, it could cause them to rethink their position on giving you another chance at custody."

"You let me worry about the Handcocks. And if you would stop fuming for a second, you'd see the value of what I'm suggesting. Think about it, Katie. I'd be the perfect ploy. It's common knowledge in the business that I let my own company run down. I'm in the black now, yes, but if I dropped the right words to the right people, it wouldn't take much to convince them I'm still on shaky ground and in deep financial trouble."

"Be that as it may, your reputation is spotless," she argued. "Your ethics have never been in question. They wouldn't buy it."

"Don't bet on it. Those who have already fallen into the corruption-for-fun-and-profit trap are always eager to drag someone else down with them. Takes the edge off their own guilt."

"No," she said again, firmly shaking her head, determined to ignore the wisdom of his plan.

He met her eyes levelly. "I'd bet money your editor would think it would work."

"My editor? You'd actually speak with Margaret about this?"

He didn't back down an inch. "Someone has to look out for you."

"I don't believe you'd do that."

"Believe it. And believe this." He rose to his feet and met her nose-to-nose. "I care about you, deeply, and I'm damn tired of pussyfooting around that fact. Now you can run, and you can hide, and you can deny it until the cows come home. What you can't do is make it go away. And you can't count me out. I'm in, Katie. I need to see you through this one."

Her heart was starting to feel a little mushy. Her head too. "I can handle it without getting you involved."

"Maybe I *want* to be involved," he countered stubbornly. "My concern for you aside, I've had a bellyful of Brackman's greed. And you can blame yourself for my own consciousness-raising. You made me realize I'm as guilty as he is if I continue to turn a blind eye to his dealings. He's a cancer in my industry and I want— no, I *need*—to play a part in his extinction. If you won't let me do it for you, let me do it for myself."

Love for him outweighed her anger at his interference. The foolish, foolish man. He'd insisted he was in. He was in, all right. In over his head, and she was the only one who could save him.

"Appealing to my sense of duty, Ace? That's dirty pool."

He smiled, sensing, as she wanted him to, that she was weakening. "All's fair and all that."

"And all that," she agreed, and let him pull her into his arms.

"Let me help, Katie," he said softly.

She pretended to consider. She had to protect him and needed time to figure out how to keep him out of this mess. "Will you give me a week or two to think about it before I knuckle under and let you have your way?"

She felt a sigh of relief eddy through his big body.

"You got it," he said, gracious in what he thought was his victory. "As long as you let me have my way with you tonight." A nudge of his hips against hers emphasized his intentions.

Convinced she'd bought herself some time, she relaxed against him and answered his nudge with her own. "I'd like nothing better . . . but aren't you forgetting something?"

He frowned.

"Joey?" she said with a hint of a smile.

"Ah, yes. There is Joey to consider, isn't there? How 'bout we make good on my threat tomorrow night?"

"I think I can fit it into my schedule."

"In the meantime . . . dance with me, Katie." He pulled her close. "I do like the way we slow dance together. And I do love that song."

She snuggled up against him, swaying to the gently rocking beat and the telling words of the song "Just One Look."

"That *is* all it took, you know." The feel of his lips against her hair set off a great rush of tenderness inside her. "Just one look, Katie-did, and I was a goner."

Memories of the first look made her smile. "Was it my gorgeous tangle of golden curls or the lure of all that bare skin beneath my bathrobe that did it?"

"Actually . . ." He danced her in a smart circle that ended in an arching dip. "I have this toe fetish," he confessed, setting her upright again. "I couldn't wait to get my hands on that trapped little piggy."

Hearing the smile in his voice, she gave him a quick hard squeeze. "Gosh. You say the most deviant things."

"And you talk too much." He tipped her head back, feathering the hair away from her face with his fingers. "Kiss me, Katie."

As always, with Matthew, he made the moment overshadow her fear of the future, along with all her noble thoughts about getting out of his life at the earliest possible opportunity.

"Is that a request or an order?" she asked, pulling his head down to hers.

His dark eyes sparkled. "What do you want it to be?"

"Happening," she whispered. "I want it to be happening."

With a promise on his lips and a fiery glint in his eyes, he touched his mouth to hers and began to make things happen.

Katie knew she had to work fast. Matthew was a persistent man. She couldn't stall him for long. What she had to do with the time she'd bought was come up with her own plan of action against Brackman before Matthew could stage his. There was no way she was going to let him jeopardize his chance to be with Joey for her.

She wrestled day and night with the problem, and a full week passed before she developed a viable plan to deal with Brackman. She promptly presented it to Margaret.

"I don't like it. Not even a little bit," Margaret said. "But I don't know what else to have you do. Do you really think you can pull it off?"

Katie hadn't a clue, but she wasn't about to admit it. "Of course I can pull it off. What could be more simple? I arrange a meeting, place of my choice. Brackman and Stein wouldn't dare *not* show up. I confront them, make it known I'm on to them but that I'd rather have a slice of the action than turn them in. I settle for a tiny piece of the pie and pretend I think it's a great deal. They think they're so smart for buying me off so cheaply, they agree. In the meantime, I've gotten the entire conversation on tape, which I take directly to the D.A.'s office, after which Brackman and Stein go directly to jail. I repeat, simple."

"As an atomic reactor," Margaret said skeptically, and glanced over Katie's head to the opposite corner of the room. "Did you get that, Cal?"

"Umph," Cal mumbled around a corned beef on rye. "It could work."

"See?" Katie's hopes brightened marginally.

"But I go along for backup," Cal added, wiping his mouth on a paper towel. "Don't worry about it, Kate," he assured her when he saw her frown. "I may be as big as a barn, but I blend into backgrounds beautifully. They'll never know I'm there. Neither will you. Only I will be, and that's what counts if you run into trouble."

Two nights later Katie set her plan in action and managed, with very little effort on her part, to do the unthinkable.

She got herself in trouble. Big time.

The plan had gone wrong from the word go. Brackman and Stein hadn't bought it for a minute. Oh, they'd played with her for a while, acted like they had no idea what she was talking about, even made a few threats about slander, before they'd cut to the chase. She'd run out of running room in no time.

Where the devil was Cal? she wondered. If you asked her, he was *blending* in too well. She'd rather see his huge, hulking form blasting through that warehouse door than try to figure out what shadow he was lurking under. *If* he was lurking. She had told him 1522 Second Street, hadn't she, not 2215 Fifth Street?

"Look, Mr. Brackman, Mr. Stein," she said in a voice that even to her sounded only a decibel lower than stark hysteria, "you're making a mistake—"

"You ought to know about mistakes, little lady," Brackman snarled, cutting her off as he jerked her arms behind her back. "You made a big one when you thought you could run with the big dogs."

It fleetingly crossed Katie's mind that Margaret might have some grudging admiration for Brackman's doggie metaphor. Terror, however, trampled over that notion in a heck of a hurry. She bit her lower lip to keep from crying out as he lashed her wrists painfully tight, then knotted a filthy rag over her mouth.

"Put a lid on it," he said menacingly when she tried to voice her objections through the wad of rags.

She screwed the lid on tight when she saw the gun. Who was she to argue with a Smith & Wesson?

Fighting a panic the likes of which she'd never known, she wondered what happened now. Something told her they're weren't going to take her out for ice cream.

She didn't have to wonder long. She was no match

for Brackman physically, and with her mouth gagged, what little power of reason she might have had over the fidgety Stein was lost too.

Warning her not to fight him, Brackman dragged her into what she quickly assessed was an old coal room.

That had been about an hour ago. One long hour of dark shadows and strange scurrying noises that scratched away in the corners of the pitch-black room.

Forcing herself not to think about the darkness or the noises, she strained to hear the angry grumbles of the men standing guard outside the door. All the while she shimmied and tugged with everything that was in her to break free of the chair they'd tied her to.

Fear continually threatened to paralyze her, but she worked her mouth up and down in an attempt to loosen the gag. Ignoring the taste of coal dust and dirt and the saltiness of what she suspected was her own blood, she worried the rag relentlessly. Her reward was a slight give and slide. Not enough to let her yell for help, but enough to shore up her hope.

If she just hadn't agreed to use a wire that had to be hidden in the seam of a bra. She *never* wore a bra. Her discomfort had shown. All the fidgeting and shoulder shifting had given her away. Well, she was braless again, and incensed at the crudeness with which they'd relieved her of the wire. She was also scared down to Matthew's favorite little piggies about what kind of fish might be having her à la carte about midnight.

Don't think about that now, she ordered herself. Think about how you're going to get out of this mess.

Instead she thought of Matthew and Joey, and for the first time since they'd dragged her in there, defeat dealt a crippling blow.

Darn her stupid hide. She might never see them again. The thought of the pain that would cause Matthew was devastating.

Even in this dark isolation, she could see his face. Hear his voice . . . Eyes suddenly wide, she snapped her head toward the door and listened. She *had* heard his voice. He was here, outside the door, and he was shouting her name like a wild man!

Everything happened at once then. She bounced and jerked her chair toward the door. Falling against it with a thud, she kicked and shrieked as hard and as loud as her bonds would let her.

Above the wild pounding of blood gushing through her ears, she heard the sharp report of gunfire, then the reverberations of a voice blaring through a megaphone.

"Kansas City P.D. Throw down your weapons and no one gets hurt."

And through it all, through it all, came Matthew's beautiful, angry lion's roar. "Katie!!! Katie!!!!"

"Ummmpppphhhh!!!" She screamed and groaned and banged against the door. A heartbeat later, it crashed open, Matthew's shoulder the battering ram that broke it in.

Through a mist of dirt and tears, she watched him come to her. Watched the anguish on his face fade to relief. Watched his head, as he knelt before her, bend down to better see the knots at her wrists.

Gently, with trembling hands, he freed her. Slowly, with a nightmare of emotions clouding his eyes, he pulled her into his arms. Distinctly, with no trace of hesitancy in his voice, he whispered in her ear. "When I get you home, I swear, Katie, I'm going to throttle you for the hell you've put me through."

The cry escaped then, sharp, harsh, and strangled as she wrapped herself around him as tightly as fragrance on a flower. "I was so s-scared."

"Shhh. It's okay. I've got you now." He crushed her against him, then stood with her cradled in his arms. "Come on. Let's get you home."

She buried her face against his chest, trusting him to take her there.

In thick silence Matthew watched her sleep. He dragged a hand through his hair, swore under his breath, and rose stiffly from the chair by his bed.

At the open window, he braced his palms above his head on the molding, relishing the cool, damp kiss of the night breeze as it whispered across his naked belly.

He could have lost her that night. He almost had. His gut tightened and clenched with the memory of how she'd looked when he'd finally found her, like a child cornered by the demons of the night. Like a bruised and bleeding princess abducted from her bed of feathers.

Only he was no prince come to save her. The thoughts he battled now were proof of that.

He closed his eyes, ashamed yet stunned and strangely exalted by the fierceness with which he wanted to take her.

Blood lust. For the first time in his life, he understood the meaning of the term. He fought a huge, gnawing need to make her feel the hurt she'd put him through. To show her he was lord and master and to quench all his anger toward the bastards who had hurt her.

He turned and walked slowly to the bed, gazing down on her. She looked so fragile, so vulnerable. Even more so than when he'd bathed her, washed her hair, and tended to the abrasions on her wrists and ankles and mouth. His gut knotted again, as he thought about the abuse she'd suffered.

She stirred and whispered his name in a small, frightened voice.

"I'm here, Katie."

Through the darkness, he sensed her relief.

"Come to bed," she whispered raggedly.

He closed his eyes and drew a deep breath. "I don't think that would be such a good idea right now."

The sheets rustled softly as she reached to turn on the bedside lamp. Catching the covers to her breasts, she sat up and raked the tumbling mane of damp hair from her eyes.

Desire swelled and pulsed as their gazes snagged in the shadowy light. She watched him in questioning silence.

"You're still angry," she said at last.

His silence was confirmation. Drawing a deep breath, he ignored the hurt and the helplessness glittering in her wounded eyes. At least he tried to.

"Please," she said, "come to bed."

"Leave it alone, Katie. I—I'm not in the mood to be gentle."

"You'd never hurt me."

Her trust was pure and total. It shouldn't have been.

"Just let it alone for tonight," he told her one final time.

He could see in her eyes she wasn't about to heed his warning. When she released the sheet and let it fall, he dropped his noble ideals like the excess baggage they had become.

With a groan of raw animal frustration, he went to her. Sinking one knee into the mattress, he buried his hands in her hair and dragged her up against him. The caress of her lips on his belly had him tensing like a lion about to spring.

"I'm so sorry," she whispered over and over as she pressed hungry, open-mouthed kisses across the fire she'd ignited on his skin. "So sorry."

Knotting both fists in her hair, he wrenched her head back and pierced her with his gaze. "Don't *ever* do that to me again!"

"Never," she whispered, quivering with exhaustion, the latent effects of fear . . . and with a desire that was as naked and pure as his own. "I promise."

"Damn you, Katie." Lowering his mouth to her hair, he crushed her against him. "I almost lost you."

She rose to her knees, pressing herself to him, coaxing him with her body and her hands and her mouth to come with her to the place where they could forget about what had happened. "But you didn't. You didn't lose me."

Groaning in defeat, he gave it up. He fell with her on the bed. Stretching his full weight upon her, he parted her legs and drove into her with all the fury and the fear that had made him want to rip those bastards apart for what they'd done to her.

Each deep, driving thrust coupled love with anger, heart with soul, need with desperation. But more devastating than his own need was the magnitude of hers.

She soon showed him that she needed him as fiercely as he needed her, answering his turbulent invasion with a passion that not only echoed but rivaled his own.

She cried his name, demanding her own retribution, her own expulsion of the fear that had corrupted her sense of peace.

Together they demanded. Together they took. Together they retrieved what had almost been stolen from them that night: total and complete possession of each other.

When it was over, they lay in silence, like stunned survivors, taking stock of and sorting through emotions strung like rubble in the aftermath of a storm.

Always when they came together, their passion had been total, complete, exciting. This . . . this had been primal, devastating. Katie lay weeping softly beside him. Matthew felt like weeping himself.

"You didn't hurt me," she whispered, sensing his tension and his self-directed anger. "You—you overwhelmed me."

"Yeah, well, call me crazy, but finding the woman I love bound and gagged and stuck in a dark hole with rats for company tends to push me toward the edge." He hated the bitterness in his tone but couldn't conceal it.

"Matthew—"

"Go to sleep, Katie," he said. He gentled his order by folding her in his arms. "Just go to sleep. You're exhausted. We both are. Let's talk this out in the morning."

But morning was long hours away. Matthew spent the rest of the night trying to figure out what he was going to say when it finally came.

NINE

It was still dark when a restless, irrepressible unease awakened Katie from a fitful sleep. The cool sheets beside her told her Matthew had fallen victim to the same restlessness.

She looked around for a clock as she hauled herself carefully out of bed. It was five A.M. Wrapped up in Matthew's robe, she stumbled stiffly down the hall toward the faint light shining from the direction of the kitchen.

Everything hurt. Her legs, her wrists, her pride.

Matthew, in his bare feet and blue jeans, turned slowly when he heard her pad into the kitchen. He flicked off the flame under the teakettle.

"I woke you," he said.

She shook her head.

"How are you?"

Too much worry, too much guilt crowded his eyes,

which looked as if they hadn't been closed at all that night. She needed to do something to cheer him. Only she didn't have it in her. She felt bruised and embarrassed and more in need of receiving comfort than offering it.

Ashamed, she looked away. Walking unsteadily to the cupboard, she reached for a pair of mugs with trembling hands. She didn't know how long she stood there staring at those empty cups, equating them to a future without Matthew, when she felt his solid strength behind her.

"It's okay," he whispered as he wrapped his arms around her and pulled her close. "It's okay. It's over."

She needed to be strong. For him, if not for herself. The thing was, at that moment, the only strength in sight seemed to be his. Setting the mugs down, she covered his hands with hers and leaned back against him, her eyes closed. The terror she'd felt locked in that dark room, the uncertainty of not knowing if she would live to see another day . . . it all came back to her.

"I should have listened to you," she whispered.

"Yes." He nodded against the top of her head. "You should have."

She forced herself to shake off the lingering shock. "How—how did you find me?"

He sighed heavily. "I hate to be the one to break this to you, but you're not as devious as you think. It's that face, you see." He turned her in his arms, his tired, gentle eyes searching the face in question. "It can't keep a secret. I was on to you from the beginning."

"The beginning?"

He brushed her hair back. "The beginning. I understand the convoluted workings of that wonderful mind of yours, Katie. You think I didn't know you wouldn't try to make the supreme sacrifice for me? The moment you asked me to give you a little time, I suspected what you planned to do with it."

"But only Margaret and Cal knew the details."

Tired as he was, he managed a smile.

The smile was very telling. She sighed. "They sang like birds, didn't they?"

"Big yellow canaries. They were worried about you. With reason."

She dropped her head against his chest, relishing the hard, safe warmth of him. "I thought it was a good plan."

"When you deal with trash like Brackman and Stein, there is no good plan. Only trouble. And it would have helped if you had given Cal the right address," he admonished her gruffly. "I never meant for it to get so far out of control." He shuddered. "We cut it too close, Katie. I almost lost you. I don't know if I could have handled it if that had happened."

"I know."

He hugged her closer still with a fierce tenderness.

"No. I don't think you do. I don't think you have a clue."

She held on tight, knowing she had hurt him with her deception and her daring. Knowing she would hurt him again before this was all over.

"Katie . . . we have to talk."

A world of foreboding punctuated his words, fore-shadowing what she knew was coming. He was going to tell her he couldn't deal with the way she handled her life. Couldn't deal with her causes and her reckless disregard for her own safety. That Joey needed more stability than she was willing to offer and that the Handcocks were bound to take exception to her for just that reason.

This latest stunt of hers could have jeopardized Matthew's chances at getting Joey back. Luckily, everything had turned out all right and the Handcocks would never find out that Matthew had put himself at risk to save her.

That knowledge was small consolation for losing him, for losing them both. The fact that Matthew was initiating the break was painful, but a relief. It meant she didn't have to work up the courage to get out of his and Joey's lives on her own. It meant she didn't have to tell Matthew about Carrie and watch his feelings for her fade to disgust.

"Look, Katie—"

She stiffened, bracing herself for the lecture, the

ultimatum, and the good-bye that would surely follow.

As it turned out, she didn't have to deal with that ominous hurdle . . . not yet. The phone shattered the expectant silence. She didn't know whether to be relieved or disappointed that the waiting wasn't over.

She didn't have to deal with either reaction long.

Dark, weary dread edged them out when Matthew hung up the phone and faced her.

The caller had been Lisa. She'd phoned from the TV station to warn them about the lead story coming up on the six A.M. news.

"*. . . And here with a special report from City Hall, is our Metropolitan correspondent, Mary Webster. Mary, what can you tell us about this unprecedented development?*"

Eyes glued to the TV, Katie huddled into herself on the sofa and wrapped Matthew's robe tighter around her legs. Beside her, she felt Matthew's entire body wind tight with tension as Mary filled all of Kansas City in.

"*. . . The entire city is still in shock over last night's arrest and this morning's scheduled arraignment of Councilman Walter Stein on charges of receiving corrupt payments and conspiracy. Arrested along with Councilman Stein was local electrical*" *contractor Jim Brackman, who will also be charged this morning. . . ."*

The words became muzzy after that as the reporter's face disappeared, replaced by a shot from the previous night of a snarling Brackman and a reporter-dodging Stein being ushered into the police station house. The next shot was of the warehouse where Katie had been held hostage.

She shuddered at the memory.

". . . It was here, at this abandoned warehouse, that Katherine McDonald, an investigative reporter for 'Today's Market' magazine, took the daring and heroic risk of meeting with the alleged conspirators with the intent of exposing their illegal activities. . . ."

"Oh, Lord." Katie groaned, wanting to make it all go away, yet drawn to the screen and the reporter's account of the story.

". . . This next clip, taken on the heels of Brackman and Stein's arrest, shows Ms. McDonald being carried out of the warehouse by Matthew Spencer, an independent building contractor, whose disregard for his own safety enabled him to rescue Ms. McDonald from the warehouse where she'd been bound and gagged by the alleged coconspirators. . . ."

Katie watched in shock as the camera zoomed in on a close-up of Matthew carrying her from the building. So much for some small hope of anonymity.

"Margaret," she muttered, when her editor's cool, sophisticated image was the next to appear on screen. She offered an in-depth, graphic account of the story and the events leading to the arrests. "You can always count on Margaret to be the soul of discretion . . . unless there's a chance it will sell subscriptions."

Beside her, Matthew was silent, jaw and fists clenched.

They were both numb when the piece ended and pork bellies and futures markets became the hot topic of the morning news show.

"This could get sticky," he said finally, his expression hard and unreadable.

"Sticky? If the Handcocks get wind of this . . . What am I saying? If? *If?* Unless these people live under a rock, they swallowed this broadcast along with their Froot Loops. I can hardly wait to see the morning paper."

As it turned out, she not only could have waited, she could have lived the rest of her natural life without seeing this particular issue. She wished she had a bird. With a big cage that needed a lot of lining material.

Their story made the front page. The headline read: CRUSADER KATIE KO'S CORRUPTION, and beneath it was a quarter-page picture of Matthew carrying her out of the building.

    KANSAS CITY, Missouri, (AP) — Councilman Walter Stein is to be charged this morning on federal corruption charges and returned to jail immediately without bond due to a threat he allegedly made to "start shooting people" after his arrest.

    To be arraigned with Stein is local electrical contractor Jim Brackman, an alleged party to the corruption scheme. Reports are that additional arrests may be made before the day is over in conjunction with these charges.

She read on in mounting horror as the reporter sensationalized and glamorized her bravery and Matthew's heroics, emphasizing the danger and drama and hinting that Matthew had shown recklessness in rescuing his lady fair.

"Oh, Matthew." She dropped her head back against the sofa and stared unblinking at the ceiling, envisioning the Handcocks' reaction to Matthew's involvement and the danger he had placed himself in and how that danger could have affected Joey. "What have I done?"

She didn't have to wait long to find out. Shortly after the paper arrived, Matthew received a call from his crew foreman. There was a problem on the job site that needed Matthew's immediate attention. He'd been reluctant to leave her, but in the end had gone with a stone-faced promise to finish their conversation when he returned.

When his doorbell rang half an hour later, she didn't give a second thought about answering it. She should have, though. She should have thought about it a lot.

The distinguished-looking man and woman who stood on the other side of the door gazed at her in sullen, measuring silence. They wore wealth, breeding, and accusation as if they had invented the terms and made all the rules.

Their identity was never in doubt in Katie's mind, yet blind hope formed an optimistic question while her mouth went on automatic pilot. "I don't suppose there's a chance you're selling something?"

Grant Handcock had snow-white hair, hawkish features, and surprisingly kind eyes. "I don't suppose we are," he said, fighting what Katie prayed might be the beginnings of a smile. She was in the process of pinning some hope on that almost smile when Eunice Handcock's clipped, nasal voice snapped her eyes front.

"Ms. McDonald, I presume?" Eunice's piercing gray gaze never left Katie's face.

Her life hadn't passed before her eyes the night before in the face of Brackman and Stein's threat. Her psyche had evidently been saving that peculiar pleasure for the scarier stuff. Eunice Handcock was definitely the scarier stuff.

"Mr. and Mrs. Handcock?"

Her rhetorical question wasn't dignified with an answer. Instead, Matthew's mother-in-law slowly and effectively judged Katie's appearance from tangled head to bare toes and back again, noting with a slight grimace how Matthew's oversized robe kept slipping down her shoulder.

"Come, Grant," she said. "I think perhaps we've come at an inopportune moment."

Her stiffly caustic remark reeked of disgust and innuendo.

That's when it finally stiffened up—the backbone Katie had always been accused of having too much of. She could mope and poor-me herself into the twenty-first century if she wanted to. But she couldn't let Matthew and Joey down. Katie of a thousand causes suddenly had more than enough purpose. If she could champion the faceless, nameless consumer, she could champion the man and the boy she loved more than life itself.

"Wait, please," she said when the Handcocks turned to go. "You don't want to leave until you've heard what I have to say. If you love Joey, and I know you do, you'll want to hear me out."

An hour later Katie watched them drive away. Then

she did what she should have done the moment she suspected she was falling in love with Matthew Spencer. After slipping out of his house and into hers, she packed a bag, locked the door behind her, and left.

Once Matthew got over the panic, anger set in. Stark, explosive, unforgiving. Next came the determination.

She thought she could just wander into his life, then wander out again at will, did she? She thought she could just leave him there with all this love to contend with, all this loneliness? Not without an explanation, she couldn't.

Not without a fight.

It took several days for him to locate the various McDonalds of Jasper County and pin down which ones were her parents. It took a couple of phone calls to make certain that's where she'd gone.

But it took only one little boy and the look on his face when he found out Katie was gone, to get Matthew into his car and headed in her direction.

When he arrived at the farm near dusk, he found her where her mother said she'd be, in the softly shadowed interior of the spacious, whitewashed barn. She was on her knees in a pen, surrounded by crackling clean straw, a half dozen calico kittens, and the scent of sweet clover that he would forever associate as unique to her.

She'd twisted her hair into a thick French braid, covered her long legs with faded denim and her torso and arms with a soft flannel shirt. Her feelings, however, lay bare when she looked up and saw him standing there.

Eyes as bright as sapphires registered her surprise and then her hope before she raised her guard. He knew then that whatever mountains he'd moved to get there had been worth the effort. He also knew she wasn't going to make it easy, on either of them.

She looked away. Setting down a squirming kitten, she folded her hands in her lap before gathering herself and bravely meeting his eyes again.

"Hello, Matthew."

He forced himself to keep his distance. If he touched her now, he might break her, she looked that fragile.

He forced a smile. "Hello, Katie."

She fidgeted a bit. He could see she was groping for something to say and decided to make it easy on her.

"I guess this is one of those awkward moments we're always hearing about," he said. "You're wondering what to say. Wondering why I'm here. Wondering how you're going to convince me to go away."

She hesitated, then rose to her feet, brushing the straw from her bottom as she straightened. "I wouldn't think it would take too much convincing."

He nodded. "You're right. It shouldn't. Leaving without a good-bye or an 'It's been nice' should have done it. If not that, finding out you gave Margaret two weeks' notice should have soaked it. Oh, and the For Sale sign that showed up in your front yard was a nice touch too."

Her gaze, full of guilt and martyred determination, jerked to his.

"Funny thing about love, though," he continued, strapping a leash on his own hurt and anger. "It's stubborn. It hangs in there when the going gets tough."

She flinched at the verbal blow, then lifted her chin. "Well, I guess you can see what happens to me when it gets tough. I cut out. I wouldn't call that too dependable, would you?"

"What I'd call it is scared."

The tensing of her shoulders told him he'd hit the nail dead center. The stubborn set of that beautiful chin told him she wasn't going to admit it anytime soon.

"It doesn't matter what you call it," she said. "Bottom line, you can't count on me. I tried to tell you that from the beginning."

He shook his head. "No, Katie, what you tried to tell me was that you weren't worth the effort. My mistake was in not reading between the lines and in not realizing how uncertain you were of my feelings . . . and of your own worth."

She looked away again, and he knew she was battling both his conclusions and her tears.

"Katie." Giving up, he went to her, grasping her shoulders, forcing himself to keep his hold light. Weary but determined, she looked up at him before she pulled out of his arms.

"It could never work for us, Matthew. The Brackman fiasco is the perfect example. I put you at risk, and in the process I put your future with Joey at risk. I can't live with that kind of guilt . . . but I can't change the way I am either. I'm a crusader. I get overinvolved. Don't ask me why. I don't know why. I just know I can't change who I am or what I feel or what I need to do."

"Have I ever asked you to change?" He heard the frustration in his voice but couldn't curb it. "Well, have I? When are you going to start paying attention? When are you going to realize I want you just the way you are? I want to love you and cherish you and yes, dammit, protect you—from yourself if I have to. I'm in this for the long haul, Katie, and what that means is that I'm willing to get involved too."

"That involvement could cost you Joey."

Fighting down the urge to shake her until her teeth rattled, he threw his head back and drew a calming breath. "Okay, let's talk about Joey. He loves you. He misses you. How do you propose to rationalize what your leaving did to him?"

That barb hit the mark. He was sorry if he hurt her, but if that's what it took to make her listen, he'd make himself do it again.

"My leaving," she said in a voice stripped of emotion, "was supposed to ensure you'd regain permanent custody of him."

"Oh, yeah. How could I have forgotten? Grant and Eunice told me about your mini-filibuster. Did you honestly think they'd believe we were just friends?"

Her frown was almost comical, it was so full of surprise. "You mean they didn't?"

"Katie, you were in my house at seven in the morning. You were in my bathrobe. You were in my arms on the front page of the paper, not to mention the morning news. Hell no, they didn't believe you.

"What they did believe, though," he continued, gentling his tone, "is that you are a woman who loves and protects those she loves with the fierceness of a she-bear—even if it means lying through your teeth to accomplish your misdirected purpose." He watched her face carefully. "What they believe is that you are the woman I love and that I'm not willing to give up either you or Joey without a fight."

She looked a little cornered, a little rattled when she responded. "A fight is exactly what I left to avoid. I don't want you to have to fight for your son because of me."

"I won't have to. Eunice and Grant admire your loyalty, if not your storytelling. You charmed them, Katie. Just like you charmed me. They've sanctioned the idea of the three of us becoming a family."

She shook her head. "I don't believe it."

"Believe it. Believe this too. Even if they hadn't, it wouldn't have mattered. I wouldn't have let you go, Katie. Not on that count. You and Joey are both worth fighting for.

"So, what now?" he asked when the silence had settled and the truths he'd told her had time to soak in. "You can't hide behind that curtain any longer. You're going to have to come up with something else."

For once, she had no comeback. But he saw the panic in her eyes and suddenly realized it was the something else that was giving her the most trouble.

"Katie, please, whatever it is, whatever happened to you, whatever you did that makes you so certain you aren't worth the effort—it can't be that bad. Can't you trust me with your secret, Katie? Can't you give me the chance to decide if it's something I can or can't deal with?"

Katie saw the frustration in his gentle eyes, heard his chocolate-rich and velvet-smooth voice take on a haggard edge. *Can it be that bad?* he'd asked.

Yes, was her only answer. Yes, it was bad. And she was too much of a coward to face his reaction if she told him.

She shouldered past him, out of the pen, and walked slowly to the open barn door. The setting sun beat down relentlessly, causing her to squint against its orange-red glare. And yet she felt cold all over.

She thought back to all the things he'd told her. Love, he'd said. Cherish, he'd said. Long haul, he'd said. Each word was a pledge. His eyes held further promise.

This was not a test, she told herself. As inevitable as the slowly sinking sun, this man and this moment were the real thing. This was his life and what she said was going to affect it from this point on.

"Katie, what are you so afraid of?"

Of your pity, she railed silently. Of seeing the love in your eyes turn to disgust if you knew the truth. She flinched when he grasped her arm and turned her to face him. His piercing gaze tore her heart apart.

"Katie, I love you—and unless you tell me you don't feel the same about me, I'm *not* going to back away from this."

She knew then just how much of a coward she was. She made herself meet his eyes. "This is hard. You—you've forced me to say what I really didn't want to say. But the truth is, you crowd me, Matthew. This—this talk of love . . . It was never supposed to go that far."

For the rest of her life she would remember the look on his face. He didn't want to believe her. And even though it was a lie, she had to make sure he did.

He stared at her long and hard. Anger, harsh and cutting, disbelief, pure and undisguised, grappled with the pain he couldn't hide.

"I'm sorry," she whispered, knowing the brevity of

her comment would lend more believability than a lengthy denial. And because if she tried to say more, she knew she'd cry like a baby.

"You're sorry," he echoed, bitterness crowding his tone. "What you are, Katie, is a very sorry liar. And you make me sorry too. I can't deal with this if you won't deal with it yourself."

He brushed past her as he strode out the door. She braced herself when he stopped and faced her one last time. "Hide out here as long as you need to. Or run as far as you think you need to go. I can't make you trust me. That's something you're going to have to decide for yourself."

He paused and shook his head, smiling without humor. "You know, it's really ironic. You've given me back so many things. I owe you for that and you refuse to let me repay you."

She stared at him blankly. "I don't understand."

"No, you don't." He paused as if debating his next words. "Maybe it's time you do. I never wanted to fall in love with you, Katie. In the beginning, I hid behind the same smoke screen you did—fear of losing Joey. But that wasn't the real issue and we both knew it.

"What scared the living blood right out of me was the prospect of *feeling* again. For four years that part of me, the feeling part, had been like a nerve that had been severed, or a jaw shot with Novocain. Numb. I'd convinced myself that numb was a helluva lot better than going through the pain of letting myself feel again. And I was afraid. Carol had been physically gone for four years, but emotionally I still wasn't ready to let her go. I didn't want her *not* to be a part of my life. That's why Lisa felt so comfortable. She was safe. She didn't stir those emotions or threaten my memories."

His dark gaze shot straight to her heart. "Then I met you, and suddenly numb just didn't cut it anymore."

He walked back to her, tipped her face to his, and brushed away the tear tracking down her cheek. "Carol will always be a part of me, but I know now that part belongs in my past. Just as whatever is keeping you from confiding in me belongs in yours.

"I want you in my future, Katie. You're the only thing keeping us from having one together. Don't . . . please don't throw it away because you're afraid to trust in what we could have."

Then he turned and walked away.

Like the thunder rumbling in the background of the midnight storm, Matthew's words rumbled over and over in Katie's head. She stared at the ceiling of her childhood bedroom and listened until she finally heard every word. It took long enough, McDonald, she blasted herself finally. But I think you've finally got it. He meant everything he said.

Until that moment, she hadn't wanted to believe he could truly want her the way she was. To believe meant she had to do some accepting too. What she had to accept was that she had to be willing to take a chance. On him. On the possibility that when he knew the complete truth about her, he wouldn't run for the closest door marked Exit.

He hadn't run yet. She was the one running.

He said he loved her. She finally believed him. She wasn't sure she deserved that love, or the promises that came with it, but in the darkness of her bedroom she became sure of one thing. She needed Matthew Spencer—to hold her, and kiss her, and love her again until only the moment mattered, until she made sure he knew that *he* was what mattered most of all.

And she owed it to herself to at least see if they had a chance.

Start with the trust, she told herself the next morning as she headed down the stairs. All he wanted was some trust. She kissed her parents good-bye and thanked them for putting up with her. Then she threw her suitcase in the back seat of her car and headed for Kansas City.

As soon as she got back, she checked to see if Matthew was home. When she saw a light come on in his kitchen, she stripped, drew a hot tub, and locked herself in the bathroom.

TEN

Coal would finish a pale second to the blackness of Matthew's mood when he got home from work that night.

Nothing had gone right at the work site. Joey wasn't due for another two days. Twenty-three hours had passed since he'd left Katie looking bruised and battered in the shadows of her father's barn. Her mother's smile of encouragement had long since faded, and what was left of his own optimism had worn paper-thin.

He stripped off his shirt and tossed it toward the hamper before heading to the kitchen for a cold beer. Twisting off the top, he glared out his sliding glass door with a total lack of appreciation for what promised to be a photo-perfect sunset. It was then, as he stood there brooding, that he noticed a light on in Katie's kitchen.

He lowered the bottle and stepped out onto his deck. The hope he felt filling his chest shouldn't be a factor a grown man should have to deal with. It should be reserved for randy sixteen-year-olds who couldn't separate their hormones from their hearts . . . or their heartaches.

She was back.

He was still reeling from the impact when he heard her faint cry for help drift out her open bathroom window.

Adrenaline shot through his system. He slammed his beer bottle down on the deck railing and sprinted across his yard to hers.

"Katie?" he yelled through the open window. "Are you all right?"

But for a wild and sudden sloshing sound, he received no response. The scent of sweet clover and steamy bathwater wafting from the window did little to settle him down.

"Katie, dammit. Answer me if you're in there." Good and worried now, he cocked an ear, then breathed a sign of relief when he heard her voice. "What did you say? I didn't catch that."

"I said . . ." She paused, then enunciated each word clearly. "Yes, I'm in here. And yes, I need you to get me out."

He didn't bother to ask why she needed him. With Katie, some questions supplied their own answers. Besides, he was too busy trying to decide what he was going to do to her once he got his hands on her.

"Matthew? Are you still there?"

He eyed the window, considering. Leaving her toe perpetually attached to that damn faucet was an extremely appealing idea. At least then she couldn't run away again.

"Matthew?"

The uncertainty in her voice finally set him in action. "I'll be right there."

Still wavering between a carefully cultivated anger over the fact that she had left him and wild elation that she was back, he trotted over to his house. After finding the baby oil and his Water Pik, he snagged her house key from the garage and let himself inside.

"Why did I know this would be locked?" he muttered after he'd tried her bathroom door.

"Sorry," she said, before he could ask why she bothered locking herself in a room in a house that was already locked. "Guess you'll have to get your tools again."

He stood back and eyed the door. Putting all his weight behind his foot, he gave the door a mighty kick. It flew open, cracking hard against the wall.

"Guess not," he said, and stalked into the room.

From behind the marginal protection of her bubbles and a soggy washcloth, Katie snapped her gaze from him to the door, which was hanging crookedly on a splintered molding. "Was that really necessary?" she asked a bit breathlessly.

He thought back to the day he'd had, to the week of pure hell since she'd left him, and the testosterone rush that had prompted his Conan the Barbarian attack on her locked door.

"Yeah," he said, meeting her eyes and daring her to dispute him. "It was necessary."

It was also necessary to take a deep breath and count backward from one hundred. Slowly. Love, relief, and anger were so tangled together, he wasn't sure if he wanted to kiss her senseless or toss her over his shoulder and see how much pink he could put into her bare bottom with the flat of his hand.

When the silence seemed on the verge of crowding him out of the tiny bathroom, he forced himself to assess the situation calmly.

"So," he said, after a lengthy and thorough appraisal of her bubble-beaded body, "any particular reason you let me think your toe was stuck in the faucet again?"

After another quick, nervous glance at her broken door, she sank lower in the water. "It seemed like a good idea at the time. Weeellll . . ." she added, looking a bit panicked when she read the warning in his dark scowl. "Would you have come to my rescue if it wasn't?"

Crossing his arms over his chest, he leaned back against the vanity. He had no intention of making this easy for her. "I guess that depends on what you needed saving from."

A downward sweep of her lashes shielded her big baby blues for a moment before she mustered the courage to look him in the eye. Then she rose, wet and slippery and suddenly brazenly wanton. "Myself. I needed saving from myself."

He swallowed thickly and wondered just which one of them needed saving the most. Holding her gaze, he willed himself to hang on to his anger, to stay hard and unbendable. When she stepped out of the tub, moving slowly and provocatively toward him, he had to settle for two out of three. His body simply wasn't willing to comply with the anger part of his strategy.

A smart man would have made her sweat—even when she plastered her sweet-smelling self against him.

A smart man would have set her away from him and told her she had a lot of nerve dragging him through hell, then thinking she could make him forget the pain with the delicate pressure of her bare breasts rubbing against him. The delicious feel of her bare bottom filling his calloused hands.

Then again, a smart man knew when to press his advantage. Which Matthew did . . . along with all the pressing she was doing.

"Are you back for good?" he asked, trying for a growl as he pulled her tighter against him.

"Yes," she whispered between random, hungry kisses.

"Are you—"

A deep, drugging kiss cut him off. He managed only to groan into her mouth, and for some reason, he forgot all the questions . . . just like he forgot that he hadn't decided to forgive her just yet.

It might have been because of the way she moved against him, or because of all that wet, silken skin, or the liquid fire of her open mouth. Or maybe it was because of the way she walked him backward into her bedroom and tumbled with him onto the bed.

It might have been a lot of things. But what it was, he realized as he let her have her way with him, was love.

It was nearing midnight when their passion had been thoroughly spent. Exhausted, elated that she was in his arms again, Katie snuggled closer, counting his heavy heartbeats as they thrummed steadily against her breast. She listened to the solid strength of them, listened to the silence in the room, and argued with her doubt.

Though he was quiet, she knew he was awake. And waiting.

As it turned out, he'd been right. She realized now that real love started with trust. He was trusting her to tell him her secret. It was time she rewarded him for waiting.

She'd weighed and measured over a hundred times

in her mind how she was going to manage it. In the end she just blurted out the words she'd been guarding for so long.

"I had a baby once." Her heart stopped along with her breath as her statement seemed to ricochet off the dark walls like an echo reminding her of her guilt.

She waited for the hand that had been idly stroking her back to resume its rhythmic cadence. When it did, she drew a relieved breath.

"Is that where you got the scar?"

The acceptance in his voice, the gentleness of his touch, the familiar warmth of his breath feathering across the top of her head gave her courage.

"C-section," she said quietly, reliving for a moment how frightened she'd been that night, how alone, and how terrified she'd been for the baby.

She felt him swallow and tense before he gathered her closer. "Did you lose the baby, Katie?"

The concern in his voice loosed the tears she'd been so determined to keep under wraps. She shook her head and knuckled them away, damning her sudden weakness.

"She—she was a little girl. I named her Carrie. She was . . . she was so pretty."

She stopped to gather herself when she heard the longing in her voice. Drawing a deep breath, she began again, determined to lay it all out for him.

"I was twenty when she was conceived. Head over

heels in love with the BMOC. Only it turned out the big man on campus wasn't so big when it came to responsibility and commitment. Especially when it involved committing to the radical of the campus and to a complication that ended in a tax dependent he was going to have to get a summer job to help support."

The hand on her back stilled. "He ran out on you?"

"Yeah, he ran. I carried the tread from his tennis shoes on my back for months."

He shook her gently. "Don't. Don't try to make a joke out of something that had to be devastating to you. He was a bastard. And you were too young to be so alone."

"Young and stupid." She thought back to that time, how she'd thought she could tackle the world and come out on top. "I was so certain I could handle it all. The birth, the baby, my studies."

"I'm sure you did handle it."

She made a sound of self-disgust. "I handled nothing. If—if I'd handled it—" Her voice broke and she had to stop, then start again.

"One night . . ." She faltered, then forced herself to continue. "One night, she went to sleep and she—she just never woke up. She'd just had her six-month birthday."

Racing to get past the pain of the memory and replaying the helpless sense of loss, the denial that a little body so perfect and pink could leave her like that, she stumbled over the words, trying to outrun the guilt that raged and accused and swore it was her fault.

"If I'd been there in the room with her, if I'd heard her cry. If I'd checked on her just once during the night, if—if I'd known what to do . . ." She heard the hysteria in her tone and fought to control it. "I thought I was so smart, but I didn't know what I was doing. If I had, Carrie would be alive today."

She stopped suddenly, aware for the first time that Matthew had raised up on an elbow and was looking down at her, smoothing the hair back from her face. She met his eyes in the darkness, confused by what she saw in them.

"Don't you see?" she said. "It was my fault she died."

"Katie, no. What happened to your baby couldn't have been your fault."

She didn't deserve the compassion in his voice. She needed to make him understand that. "The doctors tried to tell me that too. Sudden Infant Death Syndrome, they called it. SIDS. You know, they've got an acronym for everything . . . an explanation for nothing."

"There was nothing you could have done to save her."

"I was her mother. I should have known something was wrong. I should have seen some sign."

The last word escaped on a choked sob. She tried to

pull away from him, but he wouldn't let her go. He held her fast as she fought and trembled and battled the tears.

She hadn't let herself cry back then and she wouldn't let herself now. To cry would lend credibility to her grief. She wasn't entitled.

"Katie, I want you to listen to me. Sweetheart, are you with me?"

She pulled herself back from the memories and stared at him, wondering how he could possibly be looking at her like that—with compassion, not disgust. With love, not hate. He still didn't understand. Didn't realize what she had done.

"When Carol died," he said, "I took the same trip. I blamed myself. I told myself that if I'd been more observant, I'd have seen the changes in her. If we'd caught it sooner, treatment might have helped. If once she'd admitted she didn't feel well, I would have insisted she go to the doctor instead of letting her convince me she was just a little run-down. *If*," he continued, determined to make his point when Katie shook her head, "I hadn't been so busy with the construction contracts, I'd have dealt with what I was trying to deny—the fact that she was ill and in need of medical attention."

She shook her head again. "I know what you're trying to do. It's not the same."

He cupped her face in his hands and forced her to

look at him. "It is exactly the same, Katie. And believe me, I know all the arguments. I'm on intimate terms with guilt. And I finally realized, after four years of soul-searching, that there was nothing I could have done to save her. Just like there was nothing you could do to save your baby. Some things are simply out of our hands."

She closed her eyes. Denial rang in her ears. But love for him and the desire to believe in his acceptance wedged a thin slice of hope into her heart.

"I can help you get past this," he said. "I want to help you get past it. But you've got to want the same thing. Will you do that for me? Will you at least try to believe it wasn't your fault?"

She wanted to believe. She wanted to believe so much, the wanting fairly burst from her chest and lodged like a knot in her throat. "You are a wonderful man," she whispered, her eyes giving him his answer.

"I'm a selfish man. I want you in my life. I don't want you running away from me again. I need you. Joey needs you."

Doubt eddied and swirled around the edges of hope. "You can still say that now that you know?"

"I can say that *because* I know. Knowing what you've been through makes me love you that much more. The only thing I ask is that whatever the problem, you give me the chance to help you handle it. And that includes problems with the Brackmans and the Steins of this world."

She stared at him with wonder and love.

"And I want you to think about something else. Think about life, our life with Joey, and about what a beautiful baby you and I could make together."

His open acceptance and uncategorical invitation brought a tentative smile.

"I can wait until we work this through, Katie, but there's one thing I need from you right now. The love," he said in answer to her puzzled look. "You still haven't told me about the love. Don't you think you've kept me waiting long enough?"

"There's so much," she said. She touched a trembling hand to his cheek as belief in the idea of him and her together, forever, took root. "I don't know where to start."

"Why don't you start with the words?"

"I love you," she whispered brokenly but without a grain of hesitation. "So much."

"And don't," he said, touching his mouth to hers, "don't you ever forget it."

EPILOGUE

The wedding went off without a hitch . . . if you didn't count the fact that Katie was late. More than stylishly so.

"It was a hot lead," she told Margaret as she wriggled into the exquisite ivory sheath and stepped into satin shoes. "What did you want me to do?"

"Just what you did, dear," Margaret said as she set a delicate crown of wildflowers on Katie's head and shoved a bouquet to match into her hands. "I just wanted you to do it faster. How could you keep that man waiting?"

How, indeed, Katie thought as she walked down the white runner that stretched the length of the Handcocks' garden. Waiting for her at the end of the aisle, which was flanked by family and friends, were the two most important men in her life.

Both wore tailored black tuxedos with ivory cumberbunds and sprigs of wildflowers in their lapels.

One of them wore his pale blond hair slicked back and wrestled into place. He also wore a smidgen of grape jelly on the corner of his grin.

The other—Lord, would you look at the other, she thought with pride as she all but sprinted to his side.

The other wore a look that made promises she'd only dreamed about. And he wore a smile that made her feel warm and muzzy, and filled her with such joy she thought her heart would explode from the sheer volume of it.

"Just so you're forewarned," Matthew whispered to her after the ceremony, as he held her in his arms at the reception the Handcocks had insisted on throwing for them. "I'm not going to share you forever."

She smiled against his cheek. "I've heard of sibling rivalry, but father and son? I can't imagine why you think spending the first three days of our honeymoon at Worlds of Fun and several Royals games with Joey constitutes sharing."

"Picture this," he said, swirling her around the dance floor as the words of "When a Man Loves a Woman" drifted away to be replaced by "Only You." "Sunshine, sandy beaches, swaying palms."

"We're doing Oceans of Fun too?" she asked brightly.

"We're *doing* an isolated Caribbean island. Just you and me. No phones, no newspapers, no causes to distract the bride."

"That would be me," she said, snuggling closer.

"That would be you," he confirmed, smiling into her sassy blue eyes. "And I've got plans for you that involve the groom—that would be me—being the only consumer within a thousand miles who's in need of an advocate."

"Ah." She nodded sagely. "A working vacation."

"Oh, yes. You'll have your work cut out for you, all right. I plan on being a very active consumer." The wicked glint in his eye told her exactly what kind of consuming he had in mind.

She had cooperating in mind. "I swear on Ralph Nader's biography that you, Matthew Q. Public, will come away from the experience a very satisfied shopper."

Several days later, with Joey still regaling the Handcocks with tales of his ride on the Oriental Express, Matthew made good on his promise to take her away—and she made good on hers.

He wandered from the shower back into their bedroom and smiled at the bed and the smooth pale mound that was his wife's bare bottom parked in the middle of it.

Tropical sunlight poured through the window and danced across her skin. Sparks flickered and stirred in his chest, and lower, as he appreciated her thoroughly wanton sprawl.

For a such a slender little package, she sure knew

how to make use of mattress space. He'd learned the first weekend they'd spent together that she liked to take her half out of the middle.

He tossed his towel to the floor and eased onto the foot of the bed, content to watch, to study and learn yet more of the magic and the mystery of the woman who continued to yield one surprise after another. Every day with Katie was like Christmas as she shed her wrappings as if she were a package under attack by an eager five-year-old. One firm tug and the ribbon gave way to reveal the goodies inside.

Katie's love was busting out all over. He felt infused with it, ignited by it, and so full of his own love for her, he was still stunned by all of his discoveries. And he just kept wanting more.

She stirred. He smiled, saved from the guilt of waking her. Levering herself up on her elbows, she looked sleepily over her shoulder, down the length of her glorious back, past the gentle swell of her tidy little tush, and into his eyes.

"I'm beginning to suspect," she said between yawns as he started to suck on her toes, "that I've married a man who's nature runs a teensy bit toward the deviant."

"Ummm," he murmured, and considered another digit. "Deviant, demented, delirious—and you're responsible."

She sighed, a sound he now recognized as an expression of stark, undisguised pleasure. "Delightful."

He chuckled at how easily she gave him the response he wanted and nipped lightly at her heel. "Divine. Delicious. Delectable."

She smiled through the tumble of curls cascading over her shoulder. "De-hokey?"

The love nip turned into a bite that drew a startled yelp from the recipient.

"After all this time you still don't understand how this works," he said, smoothing his hand along the length of her slim calf, then upward to cup and caress her saucy bottom. "My verbal expression of lust is supposed to send you into a mindless sexual frenzy, not a fit of giggles."

Another giggle earned her a delicate pinch on her posterior.

"Maybe if you lost the phony French accent, your words would have more impact."

"You want impact?" His mouth trailed the track of his hands as he slid up the length of her body. "Then how about if I just show instead of tell?" he suggested as he lowered his weight over her.

She gasped when he raised to his knees behind her and, his broad hands gripping her hips, lifted her back to fit tightly against him.

"I could go for show," she whispered, adjusting her hips at his urging and arching breathlessly into his heat.

He showed her then. And showed her . . . and when it was over and they lay panting and spent and in incredible awe of their need for each other, she touched a gentle hand to his cheek.

"For the record, Ace . . ." She hesitated, as much to catch her breath as to form the words. "That was . . . de-best."

He was too tired to do anything but chuckle. Until he saw the tears crowding her lashes.

"Not just the sex," she went on as he watched the first tear fall.

"No?" He brushed the moisture from her cheek.

"No. It was . . . the love."

"Tell me about the love, Katie," he said, feeling a suspicious stinging behind his own eyes. "I never get tired of you telling me about the love."

"I don't know if I can." The look in her eyes melted his heart and his soul into one full, pulsing crush of emotion. "I don't know if I can put into words how you make me feel. How it feels to be your wife and Joey's mother.

"It hurts sometimes, this love I feel. It fills me up and makes me weak and makes me strong all at the same time. It makes me want to turn myself inside out for you, and share my wildest dreams with you. Only, you turned out to *be* my wildest dream and sometimes I have to pinch myself to make sure you're real."

Taking a page from her songbook, he pinched her lightly on her bottom. "Satisfied?"

"That you're real? In my heart, yes. Oh, yes. My

body, however," she added, a slow, sexy smile firing a teasing light in her eyes, "could always use a little more convincing."

He laughed and rolled her beneath him. "I love you, you insatiable little wanton."

"I love you too. And now that that's settled . . ." She snuggled deeper into his embrace. ". . . do you suppose we have time to get on with the body part of the convincing?"

"We have a lifetime," he said, and proceeded to convince her out of her ever-loving mind.

THE EDITOR'S CORNER

It's summertime, and nothing makes the living as easy—and exciting—as knowing that next month six terrific LOVESWEPTs are coming your way. Whether you decide to take them to the beach or your backyard hammock, these novels, written by your favorite authors, are guaranteed to give you hours of sheer pleasure.

Lynne Bryant leads the line-up with **BELIEVING HEART,** LOVESWEPT #630—and one tall, dark, and dangerously handsome hero. Duke King is head of his family's oil company, a man nobody dares to cross, so the last thing he expects is to be shanghaied by a woman! Though Marnie MacBride knows it's reckless to rescue this mogul from a kidnapping attempt single-handedly, she has no choice but to save him. When she sails off with him in her boat, she fancies herself his protector; little does she know that under the magic of a moonlit sky, serious, responsible Duke will throw caution to the wind and, like a swashbuckling pirate, lay claim to the potent pleasures of her lips. Marnie makes Duke think of a seductive sea witch, a feisty Venus, and he's captivated by the sweet magic of her spirit. He wishes he could give her a happy ending to their adventure together, but he knows he can never be what she wants most. And Marnie finds she has to risk all to heal his secret pain, to teach his heart to believe in dreams once more. Lynne has written a beautiful, shimmering love story.

With **ALL FOR QUINN**, LOVESWEPT #631, Kay Hooper ends her *Men of Mysteries Past* series on an unforgettable note—and a truly memorable hero. You've seen Quinn in action in the previous three books of the series, and if you're like any red-blooded woman, you've already lost your heart to this green-eyed prince of thieves. Morgan West certainly has, and that lands her in a bit of a pickle, since Quinn's expected to rob the Mysteries Past exhibit of priceless jewelry at the museum she runs. But how could she help falling under his sensual spell? Quinn's an international outlaw with charm, wit, and intelligence who, in the nine and a half weeks since they have met, has stolen a necklace right off her neck, given her the mocking gift of a concubine ring, then turned up on her doorstep wounded and vulnerable, trusting her with his life. Even as she's being enticed beyond reason, Quinn is chancing a perilous plan that can cost him her love. Pick up a copy and treat yourself to Kay at her absolute best!

Ruth Owen made quite a splash when Einstein, the jive-talking, TV-shopping computer from her first LOVESWEPT, **MELTDOWN,** won a special WISH (Women in Search of a Hero) award from *Romantic Times*. Well, in **SMOOTH OPERATOR,** LOVESWEPT #632, Einstein is back, and this time he has a sister computer with a problem. PINK loves to gamble, you see, and this keeps Katrina Sheffield on her toes. She's in charge of these two super-intelligent machines, and as much as the independent beauty hates to admit it, she needs help containing PINK's vice. Only one person is good enough to involve in this situation—Jack Fagen, the security whiz they call the Terminator. He's a ruthless troubleshooter, the kind of man every mother warns her daughter about, and though Kat should know better, she can't deny that his heat brands her with wildfire. When it becomes obvious that someone is trying to destroy all she's worked for, she has no choice but to rely on Jack to prove her innocence. Superbly combining humor and sensuality, Ruth delivers a must-read.

STORMY WEATHER, LOVESWEPT #633, by Gail Douglas, is an apt description for the turbulent state Mitch Canfield finds himself in from the moment Tiffany Greer enters his life. Though she isn't wearing a sarong and lei when he first catches sight of her, he knows instantly who the pretty woman is. The native Hawaiian has come to Winnipeg in the winter to check out his family's farm for her company, but she's got all the wrong clothes and no idea how cold it can be. Though he doubts she'll last long in the chilly north, he can't help feeling possessive or imagining what it would be like to cuddle with her beside a raging fire—and ignite a few of his own. It seems he's spending half his time making serious promises to himself to keep his hands off her, and the other half breaking those promises. Tiffany wants to keep her mind on business, but she's soon distracted by the cool beauty of the land around her and exhilarated by Mitch's potent kisses. Then she runs into the impenetrable barrier of his mysterious hurt, and she knows she's facing the biggest challenge of her life—to convince Mitch that his arms are the only place she'll ever feel warm again. Gail's luminous writing is simply irresistible.

If intensity is what you've come to expect from a novel by Laura Taylor, then **HEARTBREAKER,** LOVESWEPT #634, will undoubtedly satisfy you. After an explosion renders Naval Intelligence officer Micah Holbrook sightless, he turns furious, hostile, desperate to seize control of his life—and also more magnificently handsome than ever, Bliss Rowland decides. Ever since he saved her life years ago, she's compared every other man she's ever met to him, and no one has measured up. Now that he's come to the island of St. Thomas to begin his recuperation under her care, the last thing she intends to allow is for him to surrender to his fear. It's hard fighting for a man who doesn't want to fight to get better, and the storm of emotions that engulfs them both threatens to destroy her soul. Unsure of his recovery, Micah keeps pushing her away, determined to ignore his hunger to caress her silken skin and the taste of longing on her lips. Knowing that only her passion can heal his pain, Bliss dares him to be conquered by his need. Laura will touch your heart with this stunning love story.

Last, but certainly not least, in the line-up is **CON MAN** by Maris Soule, LOVESWEPT #635. As head of a foundation that provides money for worthy causes, Kurt Jones is definitely no con man, but he knows that's how Micki Bradford will think of him once she learns of his deception. It all starts when, instead of letting his usual investigator check out a prospective grant recipient, he decides he'll try undercover work himself. He arranges a meeting with expert rider Micki, then on the pretense that he's interested in finding a stable for a horse, pumps her for information . . . even as his gaze caresses her and he longs to touch her as she's never been touched. He's tempted to tell her the truth, to promise he'll never hurt her, but Micki has learned the hard way how irresistible a good-looking liar can be. As Kurt sweeps her into a steamy charade to unearth the facts, Kurt vows he'd dare any danger to win Micki's trust, and teach her to have faith in his love. Maris does nothing less than thrill you with this exciting romance.

On sale this month from Bantam are two thrilling novels of passion and intrigue. First is **LADY VALIANT** by the magnificent Suzanne Robinson, whom *Romantic Times* has described as "an author with star quality." In this mesmerizing tale of grand romantic adventure, Thea Hunt is determined to repay the kindness of Mary, Queen of Scots, by journeying to Scotland to warn her away from a treacherous marriage. But in the thick of an English forest, she suddenly finds herself set upon by thieves . . . and chased down by a golden-haired highwayman who stills her struggles—and stirs her heart—with one penetrating glance from his fiery blue eyes. As a spy in Queen Elizabeth's service, Robin St. John is prepared to despise Thea, whom he considers a traitorous wench, to enjoy her torment as he spirits her away to a castle where she'll remain until Mary Stuart is safely wed. But he finds himself desiring her more than any other woman he's ever met. As captive and captor clash, Robin vows to use his every weapon to make Thea surrender to the raging fires of his need and the rising heat of her own passion.

Lois Wolfe returns with **MASK OF NIGHT,** a tantalizing historical romance where one bewitching actress finds love and danger waiting in the wings. Katie Henslowe's prayers are answered the night wealthy railroad tycoon Julian Gates becomes her benefactor, hiring her family's ragtag acting troupe for his new theater. But no sooner has her uncertain world begun to settle down than the potent kiss of a maddeningly attractive stranger sends her reeling. Matt Dennigan is arrogant, enigmatic, and broke—reasons enough for Katie to avoid him. And when, for secret motives of his own, the mysterious rancher begins to draw her into his search for evidence again Julian, Katie tries to resist. But in Matt's heated embrace she finds herself giving in to her innermost longings, only to discover that she and Matt are trapped in a treacherous quest for justice. Against all odds they become partners in a dangerous mission that will take them from a teeming city to the wild frontier, testing the limits of their courage and turning their fiercest desires into spellbinding love. . . .

Also on sale this month, in the hardcover edition from Doubleday, is **SATIN AND STEELE** by the ever-popular Fayrene Preston. Long out of print, this is a wonderfully evocative and uniquely contemporary love story. Skye Anderson knows the joy and wonder of love, as well as the pain of its tragic loss. She's carved a new life for herself at Dallas's Hayes Corporation, finding security in a cocoon of hardworking days and lonely nights. Then her company is taken over by the legendary corporate raider James Steele, and once again Skye must face the possibility of losing everything she cares about. When Steele enlists her aid in organizing the new corporation, she's determined to prove herself worthy of the challenge. But as they work together side by side, she can't deny that she feels more than a professional interest in her new boss—and that the feeling is mutual. Soon she'll have to decide whether to let go of her desire for Steele once and for all—or to risk everything for a second chance at love.

Happy reading!

With warmest wishes,

Nita Taublib

Associate Publisher

Don't miss these exciting books by your
favorite Bantam authors

On sale in June:
LADY VALIANT
by *Suzanne Robinson*

MASK OF NIGHT
by *Lois Wolfe*

And in hardcover from Doubleday
SATIN AND STEELE
by *Fayrene Preston*

From the bestselling author of
Lady Defiant, Lady Hellfire, and
Lady Gallant . . .

Suzanne Robinson

"An author with star
quality . . . spectacularly talented."
—*Romantic Times*

Lady Valiant

*Breathtakingly talented author Suzanne Robinson spins a
richly romantic new historical romance set during the spellbinding Elizabethan era. LADY VALIANT is the passionate love story of Rob Savage—highwayman, nobleman, and
master spy—and the fiery young beauty he kidnaps.*

A tantalizing glimpse follows . . .

Thea Hunt refused to ride in the coach. Heavy, cumbersome,
and slow, it jounced her so that she nearly vomited after a few
minutes inside it. She preferred riding at the head of her party,
just behind the outriders, in spite of Nan Hobby's objections.
Hobby rode in the coach and shouted at her charge whenever
she felt Thea was riding too fast.

"Miiiiiistress!"

Thea groaned and turned her mare. There was no use trying to ignore Hobby. It only made her shout louder. As the outriders entered the next valley, Thea pulled alongside the coach. The vehicle jolted over a log, causing Hobby to disappear in a flurry of skirts and petticoats.

"Aaaoow," groaned Hobby. "Mistress, my bones, my bones."

"You could ride."

"That horrible mare you gave me can't be trusted."

"Not when you shriek at her and scare her into bolting."

"Aaaaow."

Thea pointed down the track that led into the oak-and-hazel-wooded valley. "We'll be following this road. No more spiny hills for a while."

She glanced up at the hills on either side of the valley. Steeply pitched like tent tops they posed a hazard to the wagons, loaded with chests and furniture, and to the coach. Yet she was glad to see them, for their presence meant northern England. Soon they would reach the border and Scotland. She heard the call of a lapwing in the distance and spotted a merlin overhead. The countryside seemed deserted except for their small party.

She'd insisted on taking as few servants and men-at-arms as necessary in order to travel quickly. She and Hobby were the only women and the men-at-arms numbered only seven including her steward. Still, the baggage and Hobby slowed them down, and she had need of haste.

The Queen of Scots was to marry that fool Darnley. When Grandmother told her the news, at first she hadn't believed it. Clever, beautiful, and softhearted, Her Majesty deserved better than that selfish toad. Thea had pondered long upon Grandmother's suggestion that she go to Scotland. Grandmother said Mary Stuart would listen to no criticism of Darnley, but that she might listen to Thea. After all, they had both shared quarters and tutors with the French royal children.

Thea had been honored with Mary's friendship, for both found themselves foreigners among a clutch of French children. Later, when Thea had need of much more than friendship, Mary had given her aid, had seen to it that Thea was allowed to go home.

Slapping her riding crop on her leg, Thea muttered to herself. "Don't think of it. That time is over. You'll go to Scotland for a time and then return to the country where no one can hurt you."

Nudging her mare, she resumed her place near the front of the line of horses and wagons. Only a cause of great moment could have forced her to leave her seclusion. She'd made her own life far away from any young noblemen. Some called her a hermit. Some accused her of false pride. None suspected the mortal wound she nursed in secret—a wound so grievous and humiliating it had sent her flying from the French court determined to quit the society of the highborn forever.

Her steward interrupted her thoughts. "Mistress, it's close to midday. Shall I look for a place to stop?"

She nodded and the man trotted ahead. Hunger had crept up on her unnoticed, and she tugged at the collar of her riding gown. Her finger caught the edge of one of the gold buttons that ran down the garment, and she felt a sting. Grimacing, she looked at her forefinger. Blood beaded up in a small cut on the side. She sucked the wound and vowed to demand that Hobby remove the buttons. They'd been a gift from Grandmother, but one of them had a sharp edge that needed filing.

It was a good excuse to replace them with the old, plainer buttons she preferred. These were too ornate for her taste. She always felt she should be wearing brocade or velvet with them, and a riding hat, which she detested. Only this morning Hobby had tried to convince her to wear one of those silly jeweled and feathered contrivances on her head. Refusing, she'd stuffed her thick black hair into a net that kept the straight locks out of her way.

She examined her finger. It had stopped bleeding. Pulling her gloves from her belt, she drew them on and searched the path ahead for signs of the steward's return. As she looked past the first outrider, something dropped on the man from the overhanging branches like an enormous fruit with appendages. The second outrider dropped under the weight of another missile and at the same time she heard shouts and grunts from the man behind her.

"Aaaaow! Murder, murder!"

A giant attacked the coach, lumbering over to it and thrusting his arms inside. A scrawny man in a patched cloak toppled into her path as she turned her horse toward the coach. He sprang erect and pointed at her.

"Here, Robin!"

She looked in the direction of the man's gaze and saw a black stallion wheel, his great bulk easily controlled by a golden-haired man who seemed a part of the animal. The stallion and his rider jumped into motion, hooves tearing the earth, the man's long body aligning itself over the horse's neck. Stilled by fright, she watched him control the animal with a strength that seemed to rival that of the stallion.

The brief stillness vanished as she understood that the man who was more stallion than human was coming for her. Fear lanced through her. She kicked her mare hard and sprang away, racing down the path through the trees. Riding sidesaddle, she had a precarious perch, but she tapped her mare with the crop, knowing that the risk of capture by a highwayman outweighed the risk of a fall. Her heart pounding with the hoofbeats of her mare, she fled.

The path twisted to the right and she nearly lost her seat as she rounded the turn. Righting herself, she felt the mare stretch her legs out and saw that the way had straightened. She leaned over her horse, not daring to look behind and lose her balance. Thus she only heard the thunder of hooves and felt the spray of dirt as the stallion caught up. The animal's black head appeared, and she kicked her mare in desperation.

A gloved hand appeared, then a golden head. An arm snaked out and encircled her waist. Thea sailed out of the saddle and landed in front of the highwayman. Terror gave her strength. She wriggled and pounded the imprisoning arm.

"None of that, beastly papist gentry mort."

Understanding little of this, caring not at all, Thea wriggled harder and managed to twist so that she could bite the highwayman's arm. She was rewarded with a howl. Twisting again, she bit the hand that snatched at her hair and thrust herself out of the saddle as the stallion was slowing to a trot.

She landed on her side, rolled, and scrambled to her feet. Ahead she could see her mare walking down the trail in search of grass. Sprinting for the animal, she felt her hair come loose from its net and sail out behind her. Only a few yards and she might escape on the mare.

Too late she heard the stallion. She glanced over her shoulder to see a scowling face. She gave a little yelp as a long, lean body sailed at her. She turned to leap out of range, but the highwayman landed on her. The force of his weight jolted the air from her lungs and she fell. The ground jumped at her face. Her head banged against something. There was a moment of sharp pain and the feeling of smothering before she lost her senses altogether.

Her next thought wasn't quite a thought, for in truth there was room in her mind for little more than feeling. Her head ached. She was queasy and she couldn't summon the strength to open her eyes. She could feel her face because someone had laid a palm against her cheek. She could feel her hand, because someone was holding it.

"Wake you, my prize. I've no winding sheet to wrap you in if you die."

The words were harsh. It was the voice of thievery and rampage, the voice of a masterless man, a highwayman. Her eyes flew open at the thought and met the sun. No, not the sun, bright light filtered through a mane of long, roughly cut tresses. She shifted her gaze to the man's face and saw his lips curve into a smile of combined satisfaction and derision. She could only lie on the ground and blink at him, waiting.

He leaned toward her and she shrank away. Glaring at her, he held her so that she couldn't retreat. He came close, and she was about to scream when he touched the neck of her gown. The feel of his gloved hand on her throat took her voice from her. She began to shake. An evil smile appeared upon his lips, then she felt a tightening of her collar and a rip. She found her voice and screamed as he tore the top button from her gown. Flailing at him weakly, she drew breath to scream again, but he clamped a hand over her mouth.

"Do you want me to stuff my gloves into your mouth?"

She stared at him, trapped by his grip and the malice in his dark blue eyes.

"Do you?"

She shook her head.

"Then keep quiet."

He removed his hand and she squeezed her eyes shut, expecting him to resume his attack. When nothing happened, she peeped at him from beneath her lashes. He was regarding her with a contemptuous look, but soon transferred his gaze to the button in his palm. He pressed it between his fingers, frowned at it, then shoved it into a pouch at his belt.

"I'll have the rest of them later," he said.

Reaching for her, he stopped when she shrank from him. He hesitated, then grinned at her.

"Sit you up by yourself then."

Still waiting for him to pounce on her, she moved her arms, but when she tried to shove herself erect, she found them useless. He snorted. Gathering her in his arms, he raised her to a sitting position. She winced at the pain in her head. His hand came up to cradle her cheek and she moaned.

"If you puke on me I'll tie you face down on your horse for the ride home."

Fear gave way to anger. In spite of her pain, she shoved at his chest. To her chagrin, what she thought were mortal blows turned out to be taps.

"Aaaow! Look what you've done to my lady."

"Get you gone, you old cow. She's well and will remain so, for now. Stubb, put the maid on a horse and let's fly. No sense waiting here for company any longer."

Thea opened her eyes. The highwayman was issuing orders to his ruffians. From her position she could see the day's growth of beard on his chin and the tense cords of muscle in his neck.

"My—my men."

"Will have a long walk," he snapped.

"Leave us," she whispered, trying to sit up. "You have your booty."

The highwayman moved abruptly to kneel in front of her. Taking her by the shoulders, he pulled her so that they faced each other eye to eye.

"But Mistress Hunt, you are the booty. All the rest is fortune's addition."

"But—"

He ignored her. Standing quickly, he picked her up. Made dizzy by the sudden change, she allowed her head to drop to his shoulder. She could smell the leather of his jerkin and feel the soft cambric of his shirt. An outlaw who wore cambric shirts.

She was transferred to the arms of another ruffian, a wiry man no taller than she with a crooked nose and a belligerent expression. Her captor mounted the black stallion again and reached down.

"Give her to me."

Lifted in front of the highwayman, she was settled in his lap a great distance from the ground. The stallion danced sideways and his master put a steadying hand on the animal's neck. The stallion calmed at once.

"Now, Mistress Hunt, shall I tie your hands, or will you behave? I got no patience for foolish gentry morts who don't know better than to try outrunning horses."

Anger got the better of her. "You may be sure the next time I leave I'll take your horse."

"God's blood, woman. You take him, and I'll give you the whipping you've asked for."

His hand touched a whip tied to his saddle and she believed him. She screamed and began to struggle.

"Cease your nattering, woman."

He fastened his hand over her mouth again. His free arm wrapped around her waist. Squeezing her against his hard body, he stifled her cries. When she went limp from lack of air, he released her.

"Any more yowling and I'll gag you."

Grabbing her by the shoulders, he drew her close so that she was forced to look into his eyes. Transfixed by their scornful beauty, she remained silent.

"What say you?" he asked. "Shall I finish what I began and take all your buttons?"

Hardly able to draw breath, she hadn't the strength to move her lips.

"Answer, woman. Will you ride quietly, or fight beneath me on the ground again?"

"R—ride."

Chuckling he turned her around so that her back was to his chest and called to his men. The outlaw called Stubb rode up leading a horse carrying Hobby, and Thea twisted her head around to see if her maid fared well.

"Look here, Rob Savage," Stubb said. "If you want to scrap with the gentry mort all day, I'm going on. No telling when someone else is going to come along, and I'm not keen on another fight this day."

"Give me a strap then."

A strap. He was going to beat her. Thea gasped and rammed her elbow into Rob's stomach. She writhed and twisted, trying to escape the first blow from the lash. Rob finally trapped her by fastening his arms about her and holding her arms to her body.

"Quick, Stubb, tie her hands with the strap."

Subsiding, Thea bit her lower lip. Her struggles had been for naught. Rob's arm left her, but he shook her by the shoulders.

"Now be quiet or I'll tie you to a pack horse."

"Aaaow! Savage, Robin Savage, the highwayman. God preserve us. We're lost, lost. Oh, mistress, it's Robin Savage. He's killed hundreds of innocent souls. He kills babes and ravages their mothers and steals food from children and burns churches and dismembers clergymen and—"

Thea felt her body grow cold and heavy at the same time. She turned and glanced up at the man who held her. He was frowning at the hysterical Hobby. Suddenly he looked down at her. One of his brows lifted and he smiled slowly.

"A body's got to have a calling."

"You—you've done these things?"

"Now how's a man to remember every little trespass and sin, especially a man as busy as me?"

He grinned at her, lifted a hand to his men, and kicked the stallion. Her head was thrown back against his chest. He steadied her with an arm around her waist, but she squirmed away from him. He ignored her efforts and pulled her close as the horse sprang into a gallop. She grasped his arm with her bound hands, trying to pry it loose to no avail. It was as much use for a snail to attempt to move a boulder.

The stallion leaped over a fallen sapling and she clutched at Savage's arm. Riding a small mare was a far less alarming experience than trying to keep her seat on this black giant. She would have to wait for a chance to escape, but escape she must.

This man was a villain with a price on his head. She remembered hearing of him now. He and his band roamed the highways of England doing murder and thievery at will. Savage would appear, relieve an honest nobleman or merchant of his wealth and vanish. No sheriff or constable could find him.

As they rode, Thea mastered her fears enough to begin to think. This man wanted more than just riches and rape. If he'd only wanted these things, he could have finished his attack when he'd begun it. And it wasn't as if she were tempting to men, a beauty worth keeping. She'd found that out long ago in France. And this Savage knew her name. The mystery calmed her somewhat. Again she twisted, daring a glance at him.

"Why have you abducted me?"

He gaped at her for a moment before returning his gaze to the road ahead. "For the same reason I take any woman. For using."

He slowed the stallion and turned off the road. Plunging into the forest, they left behind the men assigned to bring the coach and wagons. Several thieves went ahead, while Stubb and the rest followed their master. Thea summoned her courage to break the silence once more.

"Why else?"

"What?"

"It can't be the only reason, to, to . . ."

"Why not?"

"You know my name. You were looking for me, not for just anyone."

"Is that so?"

"Are you going to hold me for ransom? There are far richer prizes than me."

"Ransom. Now there's a right marvelous idea. Holding a woman for ransom's a pleasureful occupation."

As he leered down at her, fear returned. Her body shook. She swallowed and spoke faintly.

"No."

There was a sharp gasp of exasperation from Savage. "Don't you be telling me what I want."

"But you can't."

His gaze ran over her face and hair. The sight appeared to anger him, for he cursed and snarled at her.

"Don't you be telling me what I can do. God's blood, woman, I could throw you down and mount you right here."

She caught her lower lip between her teeth, frozen into her own horror by his threats. He snarled at her again and turned her away from him, holding her shoulders so that she couldn't face him. Though he used only the strength of his hands, it was enough to control her, which frightened her even more.

"I could do it," he said. "I might if you don't keep quiet. Mayhap being mounted a few times would shut you up."

Thea remained silent, not daring to anger him further. She had no experience of villains. This one had hurt her. He might hurt her worse. She must take him at his word, despite her suspicion that he'd planned to hold her for ransom. She must escape. She must escape with Hobby and find her men.

They rode for several hours through fells and dales, always heading south, deeper into England. She pondered hard upon how to escape as they traveled. Freeing herself from Savage was impossible. He was too strong and wary of her after her first attempt. She might request a stop to relieve herself, but the foul man might insist upon watching her. No, she would have to wait until they stopped for the night and hope he didn't tie her down.

Her gorge rose at the thought of what he might do once they stopped. She tried to stop her body from trembling, but failed. Her own helplessness frightened her and she struggled not to let tears fall. If she didn't escape, she would fight. It seemed to be her way, to keep fighting no matter how useless the struggle.

As dusk fell they crossed a meadow and climbed a rounded hill. At the top she had a view of the countryside. Before her stretched a great forest, its trees so thick she could see nothing but an ocean of leaves.

Savage led his men down the hillside and into the forest. As they entered, the sun faded into a twilight caused by the canopy of leaves about them. Savage rode on until the twilight had almost vanished. Halting in a clearing by a noisy stream, he lifted Thea down.

She'd been on the horse so long and the hours of fear had wearied her so much that her legs buckled under her. Savage caught her, his hands coming up under her arms, and she stumbled against him. Clutching her, he swore. She looked up at him to find him glaring at her again. She caught her breath, certain he would leap upon her.

His arms tightened about her, but he didn't throw her to the ground. Instead, he stared at her. Too confused at the moment to be afraid, she stared back. Long moments passed while they gazed at each other, studying, wary, untrusting.

When he too seemed caught in a web of reverie her fears gradually eased. Eyes of gentian blue met hers and she felt a stab of pain. To her surprise, looking at him had caused the pain. Until that moment she hadn't realized a man's mere appearance could delight to the point of pain.

It was her first long look at him free of terror. Not in all her years in the fabulous court of France had she seen such a man. Even his shoulders were muscled. They were wide in contrast to his hips and he was taller than any Frenchman. He topped any of his thievish minions and yet seemed unaware of the effect of his appearance. Despite his angelic coloring, however, he had the disposition of an adder. He was scowling at her, as if something had caught him unprepared and thus annoyed him. Wariness and fear rushed to the fore again.

"Golden eyes and jet black hair. Why did you have to be so—God's blood, woman." He thrust her away from him. "Never you mind. You were right anyway, little papist. I'm after ransom."

Bewildered, she remained where she was while he stalked away from her. He turned swiftly to point at her.

"Don't you think of running. If I have to chase you and

wrestle with you again, you'll pay in any way I find amusing." He marched off to shout ill-tempered orders at his men.

Hobby trotted up to her and began untying the leather strap that bound her hands. Thea stared at Robin Savage, frightened once more and eyeing his leather-clad figure. How could she have forgotten his cruelty and appetite simply because he had a lush, well-formed body and eyes that could kindle wet leaves? She watched him disappear into the trees at the edge of the clearing, and at last she was released from the bondage of his presence.

"He's mad," she said.

"Mad, of course, he's mad," Hobby said. "He's a thief and a murderer and a ravager."

"How could God create such a man, so—so pleasing to the eye and so evil of spirit?"

"Take no fantasy about this one, mistress. He's a foul villain who'd as soon slit your throat as spit on you."

"I know." Thea bent and whispered to Hobby. "Can you run fast and long? We must fly this night. Who knows what will happen to us once he's done settling his men."

"I can run."

"Good. I'll watch for my chance and you do as well." She looked around at the men caring for horses and making a fire. Stubb watched them as he unloaded saddlebags. "For now, I must find privacy."

Hobby pointed to a place at the edge of the clearing where bushes grew thick. They walked toward it unhindered. Hobby stopped at the edge of the clearing to guard Thea's retreat. Thea plunged into the trees looking for the thickest bushes. Thrusting a low-hanging branch aside, she rounded an oak tree. A tall form blocked her way. Before she could react, she was thrust against the tree, and a man's body pressed against hers.

Robin Savage held her fast, swearing at her. She cast a frightened glance at him, but he wasn't looking at her. He was absorbed in studying her lips. His anger had faded and his expression took on a somnolent turbulence. He leaned close and whispered in her ear, sending chills down her spine.

"Running away in spite of my warnings, little papist."

Thea felt a leg shove between her thighs. His chest pressed against her breasts, causing her to pant. He stared into her eyes and murmured.

"Naughty wench. Now I'll have to punish you."

Mask of Night
by
Lois Wolfe

author of *The Schemers*

A spectacular new historical romance that combines breathtaking intrigue and suspense with breathless passion.

She was an actress who made her living spinning dreams. He was a rancher turned spy whose dreams had all been bitterly broken. Against all odds, they became partners in a dangerous mission that would take them from the teeming city to the wild frontier, testing the limits of their courage, and turning their fiercest desires into spellbinding love . . .

Read on for a taste of this unforgettable tale.

What use Gates might have for Katie was immediately apparent when Matt saw her emerge from the cloakroom in an understated emerald green gown. He made note of the dress, especially the top of it, the part that wasn't there. Nice swoop.

Real nice swoop.

Other men noticed too, as she crossed the lobby to the front desk. Matt debated following her. He was already late for dinner with the Senator, but, hell, a little more close observation couldn't hurt.

He joined her at the front desk. Her expression showed annoyance the moment she saw him, and he guessed she regretted trying to be polite to him.

"Looks like we both have business here," he said, leaning on the counter.

She turned her back on him, leaving him free to study her, the indignant thrust of her shoulders, the fragile trough of her spine. A wisp of dark golden hair had escaped its pin and rested in the curve of her neck.

"I'm here to meet my brother, Edmund Henslowe," she told the desk clerk.

The clerk went off to check the message boxes. She cocked her chin to her shoulder and sent Matt a withering look.

Hazel, he thought. Her eyes were hazel, more green than brown.

"Miss Katie Henslowe?" the clerk asked when he returned. "Mr. Henslowe wishes you to join him in his suite."

She was obviously startled. "His suite? Here?"

"Sixth floor. Number nineteen."

Six nineteen, Matt thought, looking ahead and not at her.

"Thank you." Icy, perfunctory. She was miffed.

The clerk had business at the other end of the long front desk, and they were alone for a moment.

She stood silent awhile, then turned to Matt. "Did you get all that?"

He was cautious. "What?"

"Don't play dumb. It looks too natural on you. Nice piece of news, wasn't it? The fact that my brother has a room here? Makes it seem like he has money, doesn't it? Well, let me assure you, you and whichever of our creditors you're the snoop for, Poppy does *not* have funds to make payments."

Matt played along, glancing around the opulent lobby. "This doesn't exactly look like a place for the destitute."

"I know." She backed down, stiffly. "Just, please, try to understand. My brother is here only to develop resources for the troupe. Now, I'm sure your loan department will be glad to hear that we may have the potential to resume quarterly payments." She paused. "You *are* a bank agent for Philadelphia Savings, aren't you?"

He shook his head.

"New York Fiduciary?"

"No."

"You work in the private sector, then, for an individual?"

"You could say that."

She looked away. "It's about Edmund, isn't it?"

"How'd you guess?"

Her glance took in his unfashionable attire and worn shoes. "My brother tends to attract an eclectic and, sometimes, illicit crowd."

"Which one am I? Eclectic or illicit?"

"You're a coward and a spy, and I doubt that you've got enough grapeshot in the bag to so much as fire off your name."

He looked at her for a long time. "Insults like that don't come from a lady."

"No." She held his gaze. "And they don't apply to a gentleman."

"Look, I'm not one of your brother's Jack Nasty lowlifes."

"You're not? And yet you have business here?" She studied him thoughtfully. "Are you meeting the senator then?"

Christ, how'd she know? He felt himself grow stony-faced, trying to keep reaction to a minimum.

"I remember," she went on, "seeing you waylay the distinguished senator backstage, Mr. . . . ?" She waited again for his name.

"Nasty," he said curtly. "Jack Nasty."

"I thought so."

To his surprise, she sidled close and put a hand on his arm. "Sir?" she called to the desk clerk. "My friend here has a request."

Matt tensed. What was she doing?

"Yes, sir?" the clerk asked, returning to them.

"He needs his messages," Katie interjected before Matt could speak.

"Of course." The clerk turned to Matt. "What is the name?"

Damn her.

She smiled prettily at him. "Now, come on. Don't dawdle," she said, as to a child. "You'll make us both late."

He hated being manipulated. He especially hated a woman who did it so well.

She patted his hand. "I know you've had a terrible sore throat." She turned to the clerk. "Maybe if you could just lean close, so he can whisper."

The clerk looked dubious, but obligingly leaned over the counter.

Matt felt pressure rise inside him like steam in a boiler.

"Still hurts?" she asked. "Would it be easier if you just spell it? I'm sure—"

"Dennigan!" The word shot out from between gritted teeth.

The clerk stared, astonished.

Katie removed her hand from his. "See how much better you sound when you try?" she said, then turned to the clerk. "Please check the message box for Mr. Dennigan."

Matt leaned close so no one would see him grab her wrist, grab it hard. "Dennigan," he repeated. "Matt Dennigan."

"Charmed, I'm sure."

She jerked her arm free as the clerk returned. His manner was noticeably more unctuous toward Matt. "Mr. Dennigan? It seems Senator Cahill is waiting dinner for you in the Walker Room."

"The Walker Room," Katie said. "Isn't that the salon for very private dining?"

The clerk nodded again. "Yes, ma'am. Right through the arch and turn left."

Katie looked at Matt. "Well, now, Matt, enjoy your dinner."

She was gracious in triumph, almost sweet, he thought, as she left him. She hurried to the elevator foyer. He stood a long while, watching until the accordion gate of the elevator collapsed sideways to let her on.

She had taken his amateurish game of sleuth and, in one polished play, raised the ante to life-or-death for the Senator's investigation. If she dared mention Matt Dennigan and Senator Cahill in the same breath to the cutthroat millionaire she was about to meet, the game was over. Julian Gates would run for cover and retaliate with all the congressional influence—and hired guns—his money could buy.

Jesus Christ.

SYDNEY OMARR

Now, the world's most knowledgeable astrologer, author of many books, and internationally acclaimed syndicated columnist reveals secrets about your...

THE MOST ACCURATE, IN-DEPTH FORECAST AVAILABLE BY PHONE!

- Personal Relationships
- Financial Outlook
- Career & Work
- Travel Plans
- Immediate Future

- Family
- Friends
- Dreams
- Love
- Money

Millions of people look to Sydney Omarr every day for their personal forecasts. Now, you too can have a customized extended weekly forecast from America's #1 Astrologer! Cast exclusively for your time, date and place of birth, this is the most accurate, most reliable, most in-depth personalized astrology forecast available by phone!

WEEKLY PREDICTIONS FROM AMERICA'S #1 ASTROLOGER!

1-900-903-3000
Only $1.50 Per Min. • Avg. Length Of Call 6 Min.

Call 24 hours a day, 7 days a week. You must be 18 yrs. or older to call and have a touch tone phone.

DHS1 7/93

ASTRAL MARKETING • (702) 251-1415

OFFICIAL RULES

To enter the sweepstakes below carefully follow all instructions found elsewhere in this offer.

The **Winners Classic** will award prizes with the following approximate maximum values: 1 Grand Prize: $26,500 (or $25,000 cash alternate); 1 First Prize: $3,000; 5 Second Prizes: $400 each; 35 Third Prizes: $100 each; 1,000 Fourth Prizes: $7.50 each. Total maximum retail value of Winners Classic Sweepstakes is $42,500. Some presentations of this sweepstakes may contain individual entry numbers corresponding to one or more of the aforementioned prize levels. To determine the Winners, individual entry numbers will first be compared with the winning numbers preselected by computer. For winning numbers not returned, prizes will be awarded in random drawings from among all eligible entries received. Prize choices may be offered at various levels. If a winner chooses an automobile prize, all license and registration fees, taxes, destination charges and, other expenses not offered herein are the responsibility of the winner. If a winner chooses a trip, travel must be complete within one year from the time the prize is awarded. Minors must be accompanied by an adult. Travel companion(s) must also sign release of liability. Trips are subject to space and departure availability. Certain black-out dates may apply.

The following applies to the sweepstakes named above:

No purchase necessary. You can also enter the sweepstakes by sending your name and address to: P.O. Box 508, Gibbstown, N.J. 08027. Mail each entry separately. Sweepstakes begins 6/1/93. Entries must be received by 12/30/94. Not responsible for lost, late, damaged, misdirected, illegible or postage due mail. Mechanically reproduced entries are not eligible. All entries become property of the sponsor and will not be returned.

Prize Selection/Validations: Selection of winners will be conducted no later than 5:00 PM on January 28, 1995, by an independent judging organization whose decisions are final. Random drawings will be held at 1211 Avenue of the Americas, New York, N.Y. 10036. Entrants need not be present to win. Odds of winning are determined by total number of entries received. Circulation of this sweepstakes is estimated not to exceed 200 million. All prizes are guaranteed to be awarded and delivered to winners. Winners will be notified by mail and may be required to complete an affidavit of eligibility and release of liability which must be returned within 14 days of date on notification or alternate winners will be selected in a random drawing. Any prize notification letter or any prize returned to a participating sponsor, Bantam Doubleday Dell Publishing Group, Inc., its participating divisions or subsidiaries, or the independent judging organization as undeliverable will be awarded to an alternate winner. Prizes are not transferable. No substitution for prizes except as offered or as may be necessary due to unavailability, in which case a prize of equal or greater value will be awarded. Prizes will be awarded approximately 90 days after the drawing. All taxes are the sole responsibility of the winners. Entry constitutes permission (except where prohibited by law) to use winners' names, hometowns, and likenesses for publicity purposes without further or other compensation. Prizes won by minors will be awarded in the name of parent or legal guardian.

Participation: Sweepstakes open to residents of the United States and Canada, except for the province of Quebec. Sweepstakes sponsored by Bantam Doubleday Dell Publishing Group, Inc., (BDD), 1540 Broadway, New York, NY 10036. Versions of this sweepstakes with different graphics and prize choices will be offered in conjunction with various solicitations or promotions by different subsidiaries and divisions of BDD. Where applicable, winners will have their choice of any prize offered at level won. Employees of BDD, its divisions, subsidiaries, advertising agencies, independent judging organization, and their immediate family members are not eligible.

Canadian residents, in order to win, must first correctly answer a time limited arithmetic skill testing question. Void in Puerto Rico, Quebec and wherever prohibited or restricted by law. Subject to all federal, state, local and provincial laws and regulations. For a list of major prize winners (available after 1/29/95): send a self-addressed, stamped envelope entirely separate from your entry to: Sweepstakes Winners, P.O. Box 517, Gibbstown, NJ 08027. Requests must be received by 12/30/94. DO NOT SEND ANY OTHER CORRESPONDENCE TO THIS P.O. BOX.